CRIMINAL INNOCENCE

Recent Titles by Jeffrey Ashford from Severn House

THE COST OF INNOCENCE
CRIMINAL INNOCENCE
A DANGEROUS FRIENDSHIP
DEADLY CORRUPTION
EVIDENTIALLY GUILTY
FAIR EXCHANGE IS ROBBERY
AN HONEST BETRAYAL
ILLEGAL GUILT
JIGSAW GUILT
LOOKING-GLASS JUSTICE
MURDER WILL OUT
A TRUTHFUL INJUSTICE
A WEB OF CIRCUMSTANCES

Writing as Roderic Jeffries

AN AIR OF MURDER
DEFINITELY DECEASED
AN INSTINCTIVE SOLUTION
AN INTRIGUING MURDER
MURDER DELAYED
MURDER NEEDS IMAGINATION
A QUESTION OF MOTIVE
SEEING IS DECEIVING
A SUNNY DISAPPEARANCE
SUN, SEA AND MURDER

CRIMINAL INNOCENCE

Jeffrey Ashford

This first world edition published 2010
in Great Britain and in the USA by
SEVERN HOUSE PUBLISHERS LTD of
9–15 High Street, Sutton, Surrey, England, SM1 1DF.

British Library Cataloguing in Publication Data

Ashford, Jeffrey, 1926-
  Criminal innocence.
  1. Lawyers–Fiction. 2. Murder–Investigation–Fiction.
  3. Witnesses–Fiction. 4. Threats of violence–Fiction.
  5. Conscience–Fiction. 6. Suspense fiction.
  I. Title
  823.9'14-dc22

ISBN-13: 978-0-7278-6935-7   (cased)

All Severn House titles are printed on acid-free paper.

Severn House Publishers support The Forest Stewardship Council [FSC], the
leading international forest certification organisation. All our titles that are
printed on Greenpeace-approved FSC-certified paper carry the FSC logo

Mixed Sources
Product group from well-managed
forests and other controlled sources
www.fsc.org Cert no. SA-COC-1565
© 1996 Forest Stewardship Council

Typeset by Palimpsest Book Production Ltd.,
Falkirk, Stirlingshire, Scotland.
Printed and bound in Great Britain by
MPG Books Ltd., Bodmin, Cornwall.

ONE

As Fitch watched, in the stolen BMW, the last light in No. 14 was switched off. The building, one in a row which fronted High Street in Flexford, was now in darkness. He picked up the mobile on the passenger seat with his gloved hand, dialled. It took time for the call to be answered. 'Mr Donaldson?' He suffered sharp tension as he always did before a job became active; a fact of which he was ashamed.

'What is it?'

'DC Swan, county police. I'm ringing to inform you that DC Merriman will be along very soon to have a word with you.'

'At this time of night?'

'Sorry about that, but it's important; security.'

'Has something suddenly happened?'

'DC Merriman will explain.'

'I don't know him.'

'DC Blane has moved to another division and Detective Constable Merriman has become the new security officer.'

'Look, I've had a tiring time, dealing with people who don't know their job, and I was hoping for a long sleep. Can't it wait until the morning?'

'The guv'nor, Inspector Carren, said you'd likely be in bed, but it is essential you have a word with DC Merriman.'

'I suppose then . . . Very well. I'll be ready.'

Fitch had previously worked out how long it would take a detective to prepare to leave divisional HQ and drive to where he was now. Twenty minutes. Things were going to plan. Nevertheless, he again reviewed the coming theft. Satisfied the purchase of a minor piece of jewellery when other customers were present could cause no reason for him to be remembered, he had gone into the jewellers. Donaldson, in his late sixties, of light build, had been dealing with a couple who were considering buying a pearl necklace. Were the pearls natural or cultivated? Only fools could think one might buy a rope of natural pearls for that sort of money, but Donaldson was too deferentially polite ever to infer that. The assistant, in her early twenties, had been talking to a tarty woman. As Fitch had waited, his trained eyes had noted a panic button; he assumed there would be another out of sight. The outside door was made of wood and glass; there was a steel lined inner door which could be swung round to cover it and the locks were first class. The display window was guarded by a grill and a laser beam. Forced entry from the road was clearly an absurdity. Entry into the shop from the accommodation above it would be less well guarded. He had learned the names of the police officers in divisional HQ. He had told Daisy to pose as a saleswoman for a firm which made safes and try to sell a new one to Donaldson. She had a pleasing voice, when she could be bothered, and with the help of a little female flattery had briefly persuaded him to listen to her detailing the advantages of a modern safe, the disadvantages of owning an old one. Donaldson had fussily claimed that the one in his office was of top quality, made by McCartney, and probably stronger than any safe he was being offered. When Daisy had told Fitch what had been said, Fitch had been delighted. McCartney had gone out of business many years before and their safes lacked modern innovations.

He returned the mobile, which had come with the car, to its holder. Later, it would be destroyed along with the car. He was wearing a raincoat with a broad collar, turned up as high as possible, a hat with a wide brim, turned down. On the front passenger seat was an enlarged bum bag in which were the tools he would need to force the safe – tools made by himself, which included a sectional jemmy, a drill which looked too small to be effective, yet was highly efficient, and an expanding, spring-loaded metal cosh.

He picked up the bum bag, stepped out of the car, shut the door, and fixed the bum bag around his waist. He crossed the small square towards the alleyway that provided access to High Street, from which came the occasional sounds of a car. Just before the alleyway was the outside door to the accommodation; above this was an outside light; to the right, the speaker of a call unit. He pressed the button on the cosh, which caused it to expand, reached up and smashed the light. This was the one moment when he had to trust to luck . . .

Luck was with him. There had been no late-night pedestrian turning into the alleyway, no one near enough to have been alerted by the sound of breaking glass. He pressed the button of the call unit. Upstairs, a dog barked twice. The barks suggested a large dog, and he had to assume it was a trained guard dog. He cursed his negligence. He should have accepted the possibility and brought a spray or poisoned meat.

Through the speaker, a tinny sounding voice asked, 'Who is it?'

'Detective Constable Merriman, Mr Donaldson. They said you'd be expecting me.'

'Wait.'

He tilted his head forward so that as much as possible of his face was concealed. In the centre of the door was a small spyhole. This became dimly illuminated, then almost dark again as he was viewed through it.

'Damn!'

An old-fashioned swear word from an old-fashioned man, prompted by finding the outside light would not work and enable him to view the caller clearly.

'Why are you here?'

'Inspector Carren told me to speak to you.'

'What about?'

'A matter of security.'

'You're not the usual security officer.'

'DC Blane has been moved to C division and I've taken over.'

'Can't you tell me now what the problem is?'

'It'll take a bit of time and it's not very pleasant standing out here.'

He could hear the sound of a bar being lifted. Success now depended on his getting inside within seconds.

The door began to open. He used his shoulder to slam it wide open, stepped inside. Donaldson had been sent sprawling and was on his knees. Fitch brought the cosh down on his head and he collapsed.

A dog's growling drew his attention to the head of the stairs. A giant schnauzer stood there for a moment, then raced down the stairs and leapt at Fitch. He swung the cosh and the tip struck the dog's right eye, forcing it to back off, yelping with pain.

Donaldson had managed to regain his feet and stagger across to the stairs, by the side of which was an alarm button. Fitch reached him just as he succeeded in pressing the button. An old man and a dog had ruined the attempted robbery. Wild with anger, Fitch struck once more with the cosh, then kicked the sprawling man.

The dog had overcome its pain and shock and it attacked Fitch, its mouth open. Fitch swung the cosh and this time struck truly. Not content, he hit the supine dog four times more, turning its head into a mush of bone, flesh, hair, and blood. Only then, his anger partially released, did he accept the stupidity of preferring revenge to escape.

TWO

Steven Drury walked past the notice that denied access to the car park to anyone but an employee and began to turn into the small square at the back of Sainsbury's supermarket. He had time to notice another car was now present before a man ran into him with such violence he was knocked sideways to the ground, his head hitting the concrete and his tie flying up and into his face.

He began to shout his anger. Something hit his head violently, sending spears of 'light' through his skull. Pain began to flare; a shoe thudded into his side. As he lay on the ground, he saw his assailant run round the bonnet of the other car, jerk open the driving door. The interior light came on, partially illuminating the man's face before he climbed into the car, slammed the door shut, started the engine and drove out of the square.

Drury lost consciousness.

'What's up, then?'

Drury looked up, slowly decided that a police constable was standing by his side. He tried to explain what had happened, could initially only mumble.

'Been drinking too well, have you?'

He made the mistake of shaking his head. Fresh spears of pain crossed his head.

A torch was switched on. He closed his eyes.

'I'm calling an ambulance.'

He wanted to say that wasn't necessary – he'd had an irrational fear of hospitals since his tonsils and adenoids had been removed at the age of eight – but couldn't find the words.

He heard the constable's talking, couldn't be bothered to identify what was being said.

'They're on their way.'

Who was on whose way?

'Are you married?'

What did that matter?

The constable knelt to hear and be heard. He spoke slowly. 'If you are married, we will get in touch with your wife.'

Diana wasn't at home, she was . . . where . . .? 'Abroad.'

'Is there someone here we can contact and say what's happened?'

He remembered he had a sister. He mumbled, 'Audrey.'

'How do we get in touch with her?'

At the third attempt he managed to provide her address.

Audrey Timpson had a determined character and, for much of the time, possessed little tact. She spoke to the woman behind the reception desk at Flexford General Hospital without trying to hide her impatience. 'Is someone going to tell me how my brother is *before* breakfast time?'

The receptionist had noticed Audrey's coat would probably have been rejected if offered to a charity shop; she had also seen the diamond brooch and engagement ring. Rich bitch playing rough, she judged, mistaking concern for the rudeness of supposed superiority. 'You'll be told as soon as the doctor is free to do so. Until then, you'll have to wait.'

Audrey, for once, restrained a sharp rejoinder. She crossed into the visitors' waiting area, sat, picked up a copy of the local magazine. When she put it down, she could not have said what had been the subject of the article she had been reading. She checked the time again, suffered the fear that delay meant potential disaster.

Someone approached the area. She looked up and saw a youngish man in a surgical gown whose face expressed his tiredness.

'Mrs Timpson?' he asked.

'Yes.' Her fear increased as she waited for him to speak again.

'Your brother suffered a severe blow to his head, but his skull has not been fractured. As far as we can judge at the moment, he has not suffered any damage to the brain.'

'Thank God for that!'

'As I have told him, he should stay here for the next forty-eight hours to make certain his injuries do not result in problems we have been unable immediately to uncover, but he insists on leaving.'

'He can't stand hospitals.'

'Very few patients willingly stay here.' He smiled. 'He will need to be seen tomorrow. Since I understand his wife is abroad, where will he be staying?'

'With me.'

'Then please make certain he returns tomorrow morning at eleven. And, of course, if there's the slightest cause to do so, bring him back here before then. He will probably suffer a headache for quite some time and he has been given something to try to counter that. Should it become severe, he must return here immediately.'

'I'll see he does.'

'He will be with you very shortly.'

She thanked him. Obviously, her brother should remain in hospital, but there was as much chance of persuading her barrister brother to do so as of his agreeing it was true that 'the law is a ass – a idiot'.

Drury, accompanied by a nurse, came through a doorway and over to where she stood. 'You can't keep a good man down!'

As always, she thought with the annoyance of recent fear, he was trying to make light of what had happened. 'But you *can* make him look as if he's been in a rugger scrum.'

The nurse said, 'There's every reason to hope Mr Drury will soon feel a little less battered.' She turned away, then back. 'We had to undress Mr Drury for the x-rays. I suggested, when he dressed afterwards, that he didn't bother with his tie, since it would be better for him not to restrict the neck at all. I almost forgot to hand it back.' She passed a soberly patterned tie to Audrey, who put it in the pocket of her ancient and stained coat, worn because it was the first one she had grabbed in her frantic haste to leave home.

Drury walked slowly and accepted the help of her arm. When they reached her Jaguar in the hospital car park, she opened the passenger door for him.

'A reversal of etiquette,' he remarked.

'You can forget etiquette until you're fit enough to indulge in it. Get in.'

He sat. 'I may close the door myself?'

She slammed it shut in reply. His banter was reassuring, if irksome. She settled behind the wheel, switched on engine and lights.

'It's strange how consequences often lack sequence,' he remarked.

'What's that supposed to mean?'

'Because I was with the Ackroyds for dinner and that went with such a swing, I lost all sense of time and became the guest who doesn't know when to leave. If I'd observed the etiquette of which you are so contemptuous, I'd have left them at a respectable hour and escaped a battering. But why should that be a consequence of a late, and therefore rude, departure?'

'You'll have to answer your own question.'

She engaged 'drive', backed, stopped at the entrance to allow several cars to pass.

'Would you like to take me to the car park at Sainsbury's?'

'Why?'

'My car's there and I can drive home.'

'It sounds as if you need to return to the hospital p.d.q.' She drew into the road, turned right. 'If you think you're going home to be on your own after what's happened, your brain really has been damaged. You're coming back to our place. You'll phone Diana and then have a piping hot bath in the hope that will make some common sense return.'

'I'm not certain it would be a good idea to speak to her right now. Their time is an hour ahead, so she'll be fast asleep. Waking her up and telling her I'm just back from hospital after being thumped on the head is bound to panic her, and she'll think I'm almost at death's door and she must come back on the first available flight. It'll be a shame if Wendy and she return before they'd planned to.'

'I suppose you could be half right.' She braked for red lights. 'Is their trip doing Wendy as much good as you'd both hoped?'

'When I spoke to Diana last night, she told me Wendy was a different child – running about and swimming without becoming breathless, laughing, sleeping the night through. Our doctor said it should help her health to enjoy a better climate, but we never thought it could do that so well.'

'Fingers crossed it has a lasting effect.' The lights changed to green and she drove forward. 'What a hell of a time Wendy has suffered from asthma. Did anyone in our grandparents' generation suffer seriously from it?'

'I've never heard that they did.'

'But, as everything is said to be these days, it's in the genes.'

Drury was asleep when Audrey came into the bedroom and switched on the light. 'Sorry to do this, Steve, but a uniformed policeman has just turned up to say they want your clothes. Need them for forensic examination. I asked the constable why the hell they hadn't collected them at the hospital then, and all he could say was, he couldn't answer for CID's problems. Bit of an edge there, from the sound of it. He wanted to come up and collect them himself, but I said I'd do it and try not to smear jam on anything. Didn't amuse him. Is that everything you were wearing chucked on the chair?'

'Yes.'

'Obviously, Diana still hasn't managed to explain to you what tidiness is.'

He watched her cross to one of the chairs, open out a plastic dustbin bag and put coat, trousers, shirt, underclothes, and shoes into it. 'What am I suppose to do in the morning? Walk around naked?'

'You can borrow some of Basil's clothes until you're fit enough to return home and kit yourself out.'

She switched off the light as she left. Moments later, he was asleep again.

THREE

Detective Inspector Carren watched the forensic team, in their white paper overalls, plastic gloves, and covered shoes, with masked noses and mouths, as they examined the floor, walls, and stairs, searching for bloodstains with torchlight, shone at an angle, and with ultraviolet light where luminol had been sprayed; powdering surfaces which might have recorded fingerprints; retrieving any trace which might be of consequence, recording and bagging it; photographing and videotaping. He accepted they knew their job, in some cases better than he did, yet still needed to be convinced they were missing nothing.

He was a fusser in his private life as well as his professional one. He had become very concerned when he'd started losing his hair. Failing to face reality, he had bought an expensive restorer, which promised luxurious hair regeneration, yet succeeded only in regenerating his objection to the effects of ageing. He had bought a toupee and had been gratified at his restored appearance until he had conducted the daily CID conference and had had reason to lean forward. His toupee had fallen. There had been subdued laughter. Later, he learned a DC had nicknamed him 'the man with the missing gum'.

DC Merriman came down the stairs – to the annoyance of one of the forensics, who had to move – and across to Carren. 'The news is just in, sir. Donaldson died an hour ago.'

'Hardly surprising, considering his injuries. Tell Sergeant Frenley to detail someone to find out if there's a widow.'

'His wife died some years ago.'

He was annoyed he had forgotten that, but his mind had been occupied by future actions.

He noticed that Merriman was still waiting to speak to him. 'You've met Donaldson quite often?'

'No, sir, having only just taken on security. But I've been

on to DC Blane, in C div, and he met him once a month to
check all remained well with the security in the shop. It was
always sharp, sir.'

'Do you know when was the last time Blane saw him?'

'A couple of weeks ago.'

'How did he find him?'

'Same as ever.'

'He didn't mention any problems? Someone who'd been
in his shop, behaved in a way that caught his attention, and
could have been sussing alarms and door locks?'

'No, sir.'

'So up until then, we can accept nothing had occurred to
disturb him. Did Blane mention if he thought Donaldson a
gregarious man?'

'Friendly, but rather solitary. The wife's death had hit him
hard.'

Carren rubbed the back of his neck along the edge of the
toupee – now very secure. 'There's no sign of forced entry,
so we have to presume the intruder was let into the building
by Donaldson. Why? Someone he knew and trusted? Does
Blane know the names of any of his friends?'

'Can't recall him ever mentioning anyone.'

'He was a loner?'

'Almost certainly.'

'Very well.'

Merriman left.

Carren phoned county HQ from divisional HQ, a building
of modern and therefore negligible architectural quality.
'Inspector Carren, sir. We've had a break-in at a jeweller's
in High Street, Flexford, which has resulted in the death of
the occupant, Peter Donaldson. Soon after midnight, the
alarm directly connected to this station sounded. The lads
found the ground-floor door, which gives access to the accommodation above the shop, was open. Upstairs, Donaldson,
with very severe head injuries, was lying on the floor, and
near him was his guard dog, its skull crushed. I have just
received news that Donaldson died in hospital from his
injuries.'

'I'll be with you as soon as I can.'

Carren replaced the receiver. Senior officers could be bastards, but Detective Chief Superintendent Moss was not one. He was friendly – within the relationship of senior and junior – unless there was cause not to be, when he became sharply authoritarian. There were many who believed he would make chief constable in a county force.

Carren gave orders to find out whether Drury was in a condition to be questioned.

Drury had been 'allowed' out of bed by Audrey. She was cooking a light lunch, something she might not have bothered to do had she been on her own. The phone rang. 'Can you answer it?' she called out.

'On my way.' Drury put down the newspaper, stood, walked carefully into the hall, wincing as he was reminded of the heavy bruising in his side. The telephone was on a small table in the hall, to the right of the sitting-room door.

'Constable Ingham, county police. Sorry to bother you, but can you tell me if Mr Drury is still in hospital?'

'You're speaking to him.'

'Very glad to hear you're out. Of hospital,' he added. Drury had not been discharged from a prison. 'We'd like to have a chat with you as soon as you're up to it, Mr Drury.'

'How about today?'

'That's fine. When will best suit you?'

'I'm staying for a few days with my sister, so come here?'

'That's . . .' There was a pause as Ingham read what was written on the paper in front of him. 'Broadway Manor.'

'Flat five.'

'Would five o'clock this evening be all right?'

'Yes. A word of caution. There's no parking under the flats and solid lines on either side of the road.'

'When a copper's at work, Mr Drury, the traffic wardens have learned to keep their charge forms closed.'

'Who was that?' Audrey called out as he replaced the receiver.

He crossed to the kitchen doorway, stepped inside. 'Something smells delicious.'

'It should, considering what's gone into it. Who was that?'

'A detective who wants to question me. He'll be here at five this evening. I hope that's all right with you?'

'I've shopping to do, so I'll be out of the way.' She stirred the contents of a saucepan. 'When it rang, I wondered if—' She stopped.

'Basil, bringing a dozen colleagues back for a meal?'

'Diana.'

'Why should she phone me here and not at work or at home?'

'Because . . .'

'You're sounding antagonistically guilty about something.'

'I've no reason to feel guilty. But, as a matter of fact, I did phone Diana. I thought it was wrong of you not to.'

'I told you why I didn't.'

'Typical male insensitivity. It couldn't occur to you that if she phoned you at home two or three times and there was no answer, she'd worry?'

'I often get briefed out of London and can't return the same day, maybe for two or three days.'

'If that had happened, you surely would have let her know?'

'Yes.'

'Yet now you aren't doing so? Anyway, she's not returning immediately.'

'You told her what's happened?'

'Why do you think I phoned her?'

'Yet she's not returning immediately?'

'I said it would be stupid to do so. That I was keeping a very close watch on you, the hospital is ten minutes' drive away, and if she didn't stay the whole time, Wendy couldn't gain the fullest possible benefits.'

'I'm glad she isn't. But I did think—'

'Your male ego is damaged because she isn't.'

'Sister, dear, one day your tongue will cut your lips,' he said lightly.

'You've been in the law too long to understand the value of straight speaking. One more thing. You're to ring her this evening. The number of the hotel is by the phone, since I'm sure you haven't got it with you.' She turned down one of the controls on the ceramic hob. 'I've been scaring myself.'

'That's possible?'

'Thinking what might have happened. He could have killed you. The poor jeweller has died, according to the news.'

'Luckily, he had time only to hit me the once.'

'But—'

'Remember our mother's favourite saying? What might have been is never seen.'

'I need a drink. Pour me a Cinzano – white, sweet – and whatever you want yourself.'

He left, soon returned with two filled glasses.

'Put mine down on the table, will you . . . Hell!'

'What's up?'

'The sauce has caught, despite everything.'

Life provided minor dramas along with major ones.

FOUR

Broadway Manor had been built at the turn of the century for a financier who had learned how to defraud investors with an air of honesty. Eventually, greed had resulted in a charge of fraud and a prison sentence. The house had failed to sell before World War I since people had still not learned to prefer appearance over worth, and it had been requisitioned to become a rest home for the wounded. After the war it was bought by a man who made a fortune from it, then lost all his money in the Depression. The next owner was a developer with a sufficient lack of education to know how to make a profit. Lawns, flower beds, pergola, and an artistic summer house were torn down and replaced with peas-in-the-pod houses with two and a half bedrooms, bathroom, kitchen, dining room and front room. The manor house was turned into five luxury flats. These sold as the Depression faded, and the builder congratulated himself on his business acumen. His comeuppance, assuming the necessary communication following death, was to learn that, after the turn of the century, one flat would sell for considerably more than he had received for all five.

It took Ingham time to find a parking space, and this was at the end of the road a couple of hundred yards away from Broadway Manor. Life was not meant to be smooth and easy. That morning, Jane had asked him if he expected to finish work before he had to return to work.

He walked past the row of characterless houses to the pillared and canopied entrance of the manor. There was the usual call system for multiple occupancies and he pressed the button for Flat 5.

'Who is it?'

'Constable Ingham.'

'Will you go through the hall to the left? We're on the top floor.'

The door lock buzzed. He stepped into the hall, which had

lost its original grandiosity when part of it had been incorporated into the ground-floor flat. The lift hesitated, then started with a jerk that made him look to see if there was a control button to call for help when stuck between floors. The lift came to a smooth halt.

The hallway between the two flats on that floor was of generous size; in a vase on the small spider-leg table were many red roses. Jane's favourite flower and colour . . .

Drury opened the door, asked him inside. The sitting room was furnished with quiet taste and appreciation of style; through the two sash windows, the remaining garden was visible, beyond which was a line of chestnut trees, planted to conceal the plebeian houses beyond.

Audrey came into the room and Drury introduced her. She asked if he would like coffee.

'Thank you, Mrs Timpson.'

She left.

'Let's sit, and then you tell me what exactly you want,' Drury said.

'What I'd like,' Ingham answered as he sat, 'is for you to tell me what you can remember about last night. But first, I'd better learn a few facts. You live where?'

'Parkside Farm, in Frainford. Do you know the village?'

'I'm a local, and made pocket money working on a farm nearby when I was a kid.'

'We're a mile south and alongside the Hanton Estate, hence the imaginative and incorrect name of the house.'

'You are a farmer?'

'A barrister.'

And probably a successful one, judging by his manner. 'I understand you're married?'

'My wife is in Mallorca with our daughter, Wendy, who suffers seriously from asthma. We were advised to take her to a warmer climate for a while to see if that would help.'

'I hope it has been successful?'

'She's running around without being troubled by her breathing, eating because she's hungry, not because she should.'

'That must be great for you and your wife.'

'A very early Christmas present.'

There was a brief pause, then Ingham said, 'About last night. Where were you before you returned to the car park?'

'I had dinner with friends, after coming back from London.'

'Where do they live?'

'The new block of flats in Market Street.'

'But you didn't park there?'

'It can be difficult to find a space. So, after I'd picked up my car from the station, I went into the small car park at the back of Sainsbury's, since the council car park shuts at midnight.'

'After dinner, you walked from Market Street directly towards your car?'

'Yes.'

'During this walk, did you hear anything to suggest trouble?'

'A police-car siren was sounding, but I didn't attach any immediate significance to it.'

'As you approached the car park, were you aware of a man behind you?'

'No. I was too busy thinking about Wendy to take a conscious note of what was going on around me.'

'Had you entered the car park when the man ran into you?'

'By a couple of paces at the most.'

'Then he may not have seen you before he was up to the entrance?'

'Depends on how quickly he was running. My car was to the left, so I had begun to turn in that direction.'

'What happened after you were knocked over?'

'I managed to shout – can't exactly remember what – before I was struck on the head with something very hard.'

'It was some form of cosh, probably metal. It can be a very deadly weapon.'

'Then I was lucky he was in too much of a hurry to deliver another blow.'

'How would you describe yourself at that moment?'

'Confused and wondering if my head had been split into two. Do you have any notion why this man attacked me, constable? I heard on the news that a jeweller had been murdered in the vicinity, and I confess I did wonder if I'd had a lucky escape.'

'As I understand things at the moment, there is no direct evidence to link your attacker to events at the jeweller's.'

'But there is circumstantial evidence?' Drury pressed.

'So far we know that our would-be burglar gained entrance into the property above the jeweller's shop, but the theft was frustrated when the owner's dog attacked him, giving Mr Donaldson, the victim, time to get to an alarm bell before he was further beaten. The intruder fled before police arrived on the scene. At this point in time we can only speculate whether the man who barrelled into you in such a hurry was the *same* man. However, it is certainly one of our lines of enquiry.'

'I'll help all I can, of course,' Drury said.

'It could be,' Park continued, 'that the intruder was so infuriated by his failure to rob the shop that you unfortunately provided means of releasing some of that anger, which is why he paused to try to smash your skull.'

'I hope that it failed to relieve his feelings.'

'You didn't have the chance to see him before he knocked you over?'

'No.'

'I know that the small square doesn't have its own lighting, the nearest street lamp is some way away, and by all accounts the wall cuts off most of that light, so I suppose it'll sound ridiculous to ask if you had any chance to see what he looked like after you were on the ground?'

'Not until he opened the door of his car.'

'Are you saying you did see his face?'

'When the inside light came on, it was partially visible.'

'Will you describe him?'

'I was on the ground, wondering if the world had ended, so frankly I didn't notice him all that closely.'

'Bear with me as I try to find out how much you did note. What age would you reckon he was?'

'Anything between thirty and fifty.'

'Height?'

'It wasn't possible to judge as he was leaning over, having opened the door. Then he got into the car and shut the door.'

'His build?'

'His body was little more than shadow, but I don't think he was either unusually large or small.'

'What was he wearing?'

'A hat, some kind of raincoat, but beyond that I can't say. The hat was pulled well down, the collar of the coat was raised.'

'Did his eyes draw your attention?'

'No.'

'Were his eyebrows slanting up or down? Bushy? Almost meeting each other?'

'I've no idea. I am being as much use as a pricked balloon.'

'On the contrary. What shape was his nose – small? Large? Hooked? Flat?'

'Sorry.'

'Was his chin dimpled? Square? Double?'

'I can't even swear I saw his chin.'

'Were his ears large? Small? Projecting? Laid back?'

'I think they may have been rather large.'

'Was his mouth small? Large? Slightly crooked in shape?'

'Just a mouth.'

'Any distinctive features, such as freckles, birthmarks, or tattoos?'

'I noticed none.'

Audrey entered, a tray in her hands. Drury stood, took the tray from her, put it down on the Sutherland table.

'Black or white, Mr Ingham?' she asked.

'White, please.'

'Will you help yourself to milk and sugar, so you have exactly what you want. And do try the biscuits – we think they're rather good.'

He did as asked, returned to his chair.

'So how are things going?' she asked as she sat.

Drury answered her. 'As if Mr Ingham spoke only Japanese, and I, only Peruvian.'

'Your brother is helping more than he thinks, Mrs Timpson,' Ingham said, his tone denying such optimism.

Twenty minutes later, he left. Drury accompanied him to the front door.

'Obviously, I can't describe the man,' Drury said, 'but I am reasonably sure that if I saw him again, I'd recognise him. I suppose that sounds rather unlikely?'

'Far from it. A person can remember the complete picture,

but not the individual components of it. It's supposed to be
the form of amalgamation that triggers the memory. Here's
hoping there's reason to test that theory.'

They said goodbye. Drury went into the kitchen, where
Audrey was putting cups, saucers, and plates into the dish-
washer. 'Are you free to drive me home?'

'No,' she answered sharply.

'Then I'll wait—'

'You'll wait until I reckon it'll be all right for you to be
on your own.'

'Yes, ma'am . . . I should have rung chambers before now.
Do you mind if I use your phone?'

'A damn silly question.'

He left the kitchen, returned to the sitting room, picked
up the cordless receiver and hurriedly sat. The dizziness soon
passed, but it suggested his sister might be right to refuse to
take him home.

It took him some time to remember the number of chambers. He dialled. A man answered.

'Drury here, Alec.'

'I have been expecting you to be in touch, Mr Drury.'
Rice's annoyance was obvious. 'Morrison and Trace had
been set down for this morning. Since you were not here,
and I had had no word from you, I had to say you'd been
held up in Luton with a case that had lasted far longer than
expected.'

'I was suddenly landed in hospital.' If Rice could lie, so
could he. 'And I've only a moment ago been released.'

'I trust it is nothing serious?' Rice's tone was now one of
respectful concern.

'A tap on the head from a would-be burglar. I'm OK, but
won't be up for work for a short while. You'd better pass
my briefs on until I'm back.'

'Mr Hipper will be sorry not to have you representing his
clients in two days. It was only yesterday he remarked how
smartly you had handled their last case.'

'A useful recommendation!'

'Indeed.'

'I'll be in touch the moment I have a date for returning.'

'Hopefully, that will be soon.'

He switched off the receiver. Hipper's commendation was more than a useful one, it was a gold-plated one. When a large London firm of solicitors had confidence in a barrister, briefs increased in frequency and markings.

Ingham entered the detective inspector's room and stood in front of the desk. Carren looked up.

'Mr Drury did not know a man was approaching and was knocked over without any warning. The blow to his head and kick to his stomach left him disorientated and in pain. His attacker was little more than a shadow until he opened the door of the second car in the square, the interior light came on, and Mr Drury obtained sight of the man's face.'

'A bit of luck! We have a sharp description?'

'He was wearing a hat with the brim pulled down, probably a raincoat with the collar turned up and, as I said, Drury wasn't at his sharpest.'

'You're saying he can't give a description of any use?'

'Not verbally. But he seems confident he can identify the man if he ever sees him again. There was an article in the last review from HQ about the apparent contradiction in the inability to identify detail, yet the capability to identify the whole—'

'I read it.'

'His evidence may well prove useful.'

'The recipe for dodo soup begins, first catch a dodo. His evidence isn't going to help until we can name a suspect.'

Detective Chief Superintendent Moss was staying at the Crown Hotel in the centre of Flexford. Old fashioned and offering few luxuries, it was noticeably cheaper than the two modern hotels recently built outside the town. Unlike those of politicians, police expenses were required to be as reasonable as possible.

He sat in the lounge – in need of redecoration – and slowly drank the one gin and tonic he would allow himself that evening. To date, all the right moves in the murder case had been taken – unsurprisingly, since Carren had been in command before his arrival. Not that much had been gained. A quick sighting by an injured man. Yet one could still hope that Drury would be able to recognise the murderer if he could be provisionally identified and if one was reasonably optimistic.

He finished his drink, nodded at another man with whom he had briefly spoken earlier, and made his way along a dimly lit corridor to the hotel restaurant, where he was certain not to enjoy haute cuisine.

FIVE

Ingham drove into the Tesco supermarket car park, turned off the engine, did not move. He and Jane had had a heated row the previous evening. The latest of many over the months. They had been invited to the Trumpers for dinner, and at the last moment he had had to call off because of work; she had gone on her own. By unfortunate coincidence, a similar thing had happened on their previous invitation. Louise Trumper, whose friendship was stained by inquisitiveness, had asked Jane – so Jane had informed him – if everything really was all right between her and him.

He had explained to Jane before they were married that there would be times when duty came before their social life. She had been certain that would not disturb her; she would accept the irritating situation whenever it occurred, she had said. Her acceptance had weakened with each incident and had vanished entirely when he had booked tickets at a London theatre to mark their wedding anniversary and had been called away half an hour before they were due to leave home. It was understandable that she had been bitterly disappointed, yet he could not prevent himself thinking that perhaps she . . .

He condemned himself for criticizing her, jerked his mind back to the present, and searched for and found the list of what he was to buy. Two tins of tomato soup, a bottle of cooking oil, kitchen-sink cleaner in the blue-top bottle, not the red one, two pounds of Granny Smith apples.

He left the car, entered the supermarket. She hadn't said, or he hadn't bothered to write down, which brand of soup she wanted. He chose Heinz. He moved on to domestic products. Typically, there were only red-topped bottles of sink cleaner . . .

'If it isn't Joe!'

He turned, faced a man dressed expensively. It was this sign of opulence that briefly confused him.

'Don't remember me? It's Alan.'

He remembered Alan Bradbury, even if he hadn't initially recognised him. They had both been at Harding House, the county police training college. Months into their training, several cadets had lost money. One Friday, he had found his locker door slightly ajar, and when he had brought his wallet out, it had been empty. Holding it by its edges, he had taken it to the superintendent in command, explained his loss, and hesitantly suggested it be tested for prints. Cadets were ordered to give their prints; Bradbury's were identified. His defence was weak. He had found the locker open and the wallet on the floor, had picked it up and replaced it . . . He was informed he would not be remaining in the police force.

'You look like you've just lost the family jewels,' Bradbury said jovially.

'I was surprised to see you.'

'Then if you've got over it, how about we have a noggin and a chat?'

'I'm sorry, but I'm in a bit of a rush.'

'If your boss isn't bellyaching into your mobile, it's easy to find time.'

He was curious to learn how Bradbury had gained his obvious prosperity. 'Then if it's a quick one.'

Walking through the car park, they came abreast of a Bentley Continental. Bradbury ran his hand along the end of the bonnet. 'Not a bad little car,' he said, with absurd depreciation. 'Are you running something similar?'

'A Ford.'

'Useful if you don't have to do any long-distance driving.'

'You've heard of the marque?' Ingham joked.

Bradbury laughed.

The Iron Duke had been modernized and was furnished well. There were comfortable stools in front of the bar; above, a collection of pewter tankards, each engraved with the owner's name. Four tables with chairs around them were dotted about the room, and a collection of framed prints of hunting scenes hung on the walls.

'What's your poison?' Bradbury asked as they stood by an empty stool.

'Whisky, please.'

One of the two barmen moved along to take their orders. 'Two double Laphroaigs,' Bradbury said.

'Sorry, we don't have it.'

'I'll settle for Haig,' Ingham said hastily. He would have to offer a round and did not have the money for expensive malt whiskies.

Bradbury ignored him. 'Glenlivet?'

'We've only Glenfiddich.'

'Then we'll make do with that. And a bottle of decent still water, if you have any?'

'Malvern,' the barman said curtly. He poured the whiskies and put the glasses down on the bar, then a bottle of Malvern Water.

Ingham, regretting curiosity was responsible for his being in the pub, followed Bradbury to a corner table.

'Still one of the boys in blue, Joe?' Bradbury asked.

'Yes.'

'Where d'you park your bum? On the superintendent's chair?'

'I transferred to CID.'

'Wise man. That's where there's money to be made.'

But not the kind of money he would accept, Ingham thought.

'So are you DI, DCI, or DCS?'

'DC.'

'There's a surprise! But you won't be in the ranks much longer, surely, having been a shining light at college.' He drained his glass.

'Can I get you another?'

'What say we have something to eat at the Windsor?'

The most expensive restaurant in the area. Another way of showing he was a big man, not a bumbling copper. 'I'm due home for dinner.'

'There's a pity. So much to talk about. I guess you were surprised when we met that I suggested a drink?'

'We're old acquaintances,' Ingham said weakly.

'It's because I did you shit at college.'

'You mean . . .'

'Am I admitting I nicked your money, tried to call you a

liar, and the explanation for my prints was the balls they said it was? That's right. And why do I tell you now? Conscience, old boy, sweet conscience. In the property world, without a blink I'll take someone for a couple of hundred Ks when a hundred would be generous, but ever since college, I haven't been able to forget what I did. Does me more good than you can imagine to meet you and tell you now.' He picked up their two glasses, stood.

'It's my shout.'

'But my party.'

Ingham watched Bradbury cross to the bar. Confession motivated by conscience? He would have judged conscience was a foreign word to the other.

Bradbury returned, passed across one refilled glass, and sat down. 'You're married, aren't you?'

'Yes.'

'Hard labour or cloud nine?'

'Everything's fine.'

'Kids?'

'Not yet.'

'Very wise. Little pattering feet in clodhopper boots. As a matter of fact, I'm often around here. There's room for more development in this area, which is my forte. And then there's Amy for relaxation. Talking about that, I saw you with a very attractive number some weeks back and, since you were carrying the shopping, I reckoned she had to be your wife. Wanted to say hullo, but the traffic was too thick, and by the time I was across the road, you'd disappeared.' He drank. 'As luck would have it, I saw her again the other day, only since it wasn't you with her, I didn't bother her since she wouldn't know who I was . . . Knew her temporary escort, though. That chap who runs the gymnasium. Do you know him?'

'I've met him once or twice.'

'What's his name?'

'Reginald Star.'

'Of course! Been wracking my brain to remember what someone had told me it was, but could only think of him as Don Juan – suits him better, wouldn't you say?'

'No idea.'

'Well, with all those women around him, dressed so you don't need much imagination, it would be a shame if he didn't enjoy himself. But I must admit that if Amy said she was going around with him, I'd have something to say. I mean, a chap I sometimes meet lost his wife to Juan, and it seems he wasn't the only one to learn that women like a bit of rough.'

Ingham drained his glass. 'I must be off.'

'We'll keep in touch, won't we?'

'Try to.'

'Maybe you and your wife would like to go for a sail? I've a little forty-five footer down at Lymington, and we could slip over to the Isle of Wight for a weekend.'

Ingham left, returned to his car, sat behind the wheel and stared through the windscreen. The day had started badly when Jane had pointedly remarked that there was a play, being reviewed very enthusiastically, which she'd love to see, but what was the point of trying to do so when he was bound to have to cancel the trip? Bradbury's comments had deepened the gloom. When Jane had wondered whether to join the keep-fit club, she had asked him to go with her to look at the gymnasium. He had met Star, not liked the man, and had later said so to her. His reason? She had wanted to know. Too suave, too many apparent similarities in character between him and a bigamist recently jailed. She had described his judgment as macho sneering at someone with unusually good manners. If Bradbury was right, Star did not always behave with propriety, as she had said recently – for no reason he could now recall. Yet she was a good judge of character . . .

He used back streets to cross to west Flexford, a longer but quicker route than using the major through road, which was often congested. He had bought their house with the help of money his uncle had unexpectedly left him, before house prices had reached the stratosphere. It was a house unusual only in that he had not had to take out a mortgage. Jane's car was not parked on what had once been the front garden, which now was concreted over, and he unlocked the garage and drove straight into it.

There was no note on the kitchen table to say where she

had gone, as was her habit to leave. He went into the larder, opened a bottle of lager, walked through to the front room, switched on the television, settled on the sofa and drank. The news was on. A woman had been awarded a record sum on the grounds that she had been verbally and sexually harassed at her work as a currency trader. She was shown on screen. She should have counted herself fortunate that anyone considered harassing her. Her award was five times that given to a policeman who had been paralysed when shot in the back during an attempted robbery. An age of equality meant different things to different people.

Twenty minutes later, a car drove up on to the concrete. He hurried out of the room, opened the front door.

'You're very late,' he said.

'I told you I probably would be,' Jane replied.

'You didn't.'

'I promise you, just before you left this morning, I said I might well be back late. Another husband who never listens to his wife!' Jane kissed him on the cheek. 'Does that make you feel less ignored?'

She went into the house, he followed her.

'I was very worried. I thought something must have happened to you.'

'Then I'm sorry you weren't more pleased to find that nothing had. I'll produce a quick meal as soon as I've showered.'

'Showered?'

'Stand under the thing above the bath that spurts out jets of water.'

'Why d'you need to now?'

'Because I'm sweaty.'

'Why?'

'I've been to the gym. For God's sake, do you want to know why I like to be clean?' She went up the stairs, disappeared from sight.

He hesitated, uncertain whether to say anything more, and if so, what? Yet it was very unusual for her to go to the gym in the middle of the day, especially when he would be returning for lunch. And she had *not* said she might be late.

After some time, he went upstairs. She had showered and

was in the bedroom, half dressed. Bradbury had called her
a very attractive number. She was attractive, though not
conventionally beautiful. Her light brown hair waved naturally, her eyes were deep brown, her retroussé nose matched
her mouth, which so often looked ready to smile, and her
body possessed all the right shapes and sizes . . .

'Do I pass your inspection?' she asked, before she drew
a blouse over her head.

'Why did you go to the gym?'

'Is this a survey of my lifestyle? I went because I escaped
from work early instead of late – the boss discovered he hadn't
the information he needed and it was going to take hours to
get hold of it – so I decided to enjoy a quick workout before
I returned.'

'It wasn't very quick, since you weren't here when I got
back.'

'The man has obviously had a bad morning.' She stepped
into a skirt, pulled on a sweater. 'The meal will be on the
table within ten minutes. Hopefully, in twenty minutes you'll
be able to relax.' She went past him and out of the room.

He stared at the empty doorway as he heard her go downstairs. The day before, she had remarked she had developed
a twinge in her shoulder and would probably skip a time or
two at the gym. Had that twinge suddenly vanished? She
had been mocking him for asking questions – because they
might become difficult to answer?

He went down to the kitchen. 'I met Alan Bradbury when
I was at Tesco.'

'Should I know the name?'

'He's the cadet who was flung out of Harding House for
the theft of my money.'

'Must have been an embarrassing meeting, since you were
responsible for that.'

'He was quite at ease, enjoyed telling me how successful
he'd been, how wealthy he was. He saw you with me in
town one day and tried to come across the road, but couldn't
because of the traffic.'

'Sounds like a lucky escape!'

'He saw you on another occasion.'

She put two plastic containers into the microwave.

'Meeting him seems to have disturbed you. Was it finding out that crime does pay?'

'The second time you were with Star.'

'Was the cooking time fifteen minutes or ten? I'll forget my name soon. Still, the wrapping is on the table.' She passed him, picked up one of the plastic covers, and read out loud, 'Ten.' She returned to the microwave, switched it on.

'Did you know he has a nickname?'

'Who?'

'Star.'

'I didn't. What is it? Biceps Unlimited?'

'Don Juan. Because he's always after the women who go to the gym.'

'Nonsense!'

'A friend of Bradbury lost his wife to Star.'

'Leaving a tale behind her?'

'You're deliberately misunderstanding.'

'If I knew what I'm suppose to understand, I could tell you whether it's deliberate or pure ignorance.'

'You left the gym with Star. You walked up to High Street together. Why?'

'Because we left at the same time. So what?' She studied him. 'Or do you . . . That's impossible, isn't it?'

He didn't answer.

She opened the door of the microwave, looked inside, shut it. She faced him. 'Or am I being optimistic? Are you wondering if there was anything to my walking with him, to my being back late this morning? *Are* you?'

He lost his nerve. 'Don't be silly. Is lunch ready?'

'Not quite. Are you thinking Reg is after me?'

'If he's the kind of man he is . . .'

'You can't understand that if he made a single pass at me, I'd tell him to go to hell and quit the gym, much as I like going there? You don't trust me sufficiently to know I'd immediately tell you what had happened?'

'I trust you always. But—' He stopped.

'You're wondering if I've been pumping him, rather than iron?'

'Bradbury kept hinting.'

'So now I can understand how you judge my sense of

loyalty. Who else has caught your imaginative suspicion? Mark? Bobby? Gerald? And not to forget Vincent—'

'Stop it.'

'You're not stupid, but it hasn't begun to occur to you that this man, Bradbury, saw a chance to gain revenge for what you'd done to him? If he knew how completely you've swallowed his beastly insinuations, he'd hug himself with joy.'

'It's . . . Well, things between us have been a little rocky because of my job.'

'And naturally you told him that?'

'Of course not.'

'Then he was able to strike lucky because he knew how weak you can be. I'm not hungry, so I'm going upstairs. Don't bother to come up.'

Despite her prohibition, he began to follow, then stopped. What could he say that would begin to erase his stupidity or ease her pain?

He went through to the front room, slumped down on the settee, stared into space. He heard the microwave's bell, signifying the food was cooked, and ignored it. There was the sound of movement upstairs, and he believed she was on her way down to say he had hurt her very deeply, but now that she was calmer she could understand why he had been so stupid.

She did not descend.

Twenty minutes later, dully trying to blank his thoughts, he reached over to the low coffee table and picked up a copy of the *Drigg Gazette*, which was regularly sent to Jane by her mother. Normally, he never bothered to read it. He had not lived in Cumbria and so the parochial news and articles held no interest for him, but boredom was to be far preferred to bitter self-accusation. As he turned the page, however, there was a report that, as he read it, briefly made him forget the immediate past.

SIX

The door of Carren's office was not shut, so Ingham walked in without knocking. 'Good morning, sir. You wanted me?'

Carren looked up, returned the greeting, and wondered why, on a partially sunny day, Ingham looked as if his sky was black. 'Your last report needs checking. I've noted where and why.' He sorted through the papers on his desk, found the one he wanted, and handed a computer-printed sheet of paper across. 'As soon as you like.'

'I was reading a paper last night, sir. The *Drigg Gazette*.'

'That is of interest?' he asked, annoyed by Ingham's failure to hurry away.

'I think an article in it is.'

'Then I presume it's not about fell running or Cumberland wrestling.'

'It may have a connection with the Donaldson case.'

'Explain.'

'That there was no forced entry meant Donaldson almost certainly let his attacker into the building, so Donaldson must have expected him or believed it safe to open the door. The violence makes it very unlikely the caller was a friend, however. So why should he be expected? The pizza lad, delivering supper? Not at that hour. Although we can't prove it yet, I'm working with the supposition that Donaldson and Drury's attackers are one and the same. Drury said the villain was wearing a hat with the brim pulled down and a mackintosh with the collar pulled up, which suggests he was concealing as much of his face as he could when a mask or similar was out of the question. He had to be seen, but not readily identifiable. Yet why so, if he was expected?'

'You have an answer?'

'A possibility, sir. The article in the *Drigg Gazette* concerned a thief who dressed in a copper's uniform and called at large houses in the Devil's Hillside area, saying he would like to judge what the level of security was and to give advice if it needed increasing: the incidence of thefts was rising steeply and the police were trying to help householders be protected as far as was reasonably possible. Not long after each visit, the house in question was robbed. He did very well until he visited a large place, semi-isolated, which looked an obvious mark. Unfortunately for him, the owner was a magistrate who had sent him to trial several years before and who seldom forgot a face.'

'You are suggesting our lad was dressed as a copper?'

'That seems unlikely. The time between his leaving the building and running into Drury was too short for him to have changed out of a uniform. And if he had been in uniform, Drury must surely have noticed the fact, however hazed he was.'

'I've been wondering if the man mentioned in the *Gazette* decided his scheme was shot in the north and he has come down south to find fresh pickings. As a bogus detective constable, he'd wear civilian clothes.'

Typically, Carren introduced objections in order to judge the theory's strength. 'At the time of the attempted theft, wouldn't Donaldson have refused to open up, even if he thought he was talking to a detective, and said to come back in daylight?'

'What if he had previously phoned Donaldson, posing as the DC dealing with security, and said there was reason to believe the jewellery shop had been targeted and that he needed to make a further survey of security and make certain it was A1?'

'Donaldson had met DC Blane on past surveys and knew he was the security officer.'

'It wouldn't have been difficult to tell Donaldson that DC Blane had been transferred to another department and he had taken over security.'

'How would he have known feasible names to give?'

'Phone here as a worried civilian needing advice and ask who would be along to help. If I'm right, sir, it gives us a good chance to identify the villain. The magistrate who recognized him will remember who he was; that he was recognized surely means he had previous convictions. We should be able to get mugshots and prints.'

'Accepting your surmises are correct, then where would you propose starting?'

'With the details of the bogus PC, checking if he's on our records. Since the local villains never welcome an interloper, ask them what they know as well.'

Carren leaned back in his chair and considered what he had been told, what had been suggested. 'Very well. I like your imaginative thinking.'

Ingham turned and began to walk towards the door, came to a stop as Carren said, 'Hang on.'

He turned.

Carren liked to think he ran a happy ship – one unhappy man could disturb it. 'I don't wish to pry into your personal affairs and you can tell me to mind my own business, but this morning you look as if something has gone very wrong.'

Ingham hesitated. 'I've . . . It's. . . . I've recently had to miss out on several invitations from friends and a planned trip to the theatre and that—' He stopped.

'Always causes domestic distress. A large bunch of flowers or a box of chocolates sometimes eases tension when accompanied by a full acceptance of blame, whether or not that's justified.'

He left. A carful of flowers and a dozen boxes of Jane's favourite chocolates would only result in his being reminded that attempted bribery was a moral, as well as a legal, offence.

Detective Sergeant Frenley did not see his coming retirement with the same satisfaction as did most. He enjoyed his work – the companionship, the vague sense of authority, the chance to help others, to lessen crime and its impact. Once retired, there would be no reason for anyone to be interested in what he did, to be willing to accept his advice, or to act on his suggestions. He would become a statistic. His wife was already wondering what life would be like with him around the house all day. To provide the brief change of situation that would probably be of benefit, one of them could stay with their married son for a while. But neither of them found the wife sympathetic – she knew all the answers, or rather thought she did.

The phone rang, bringing his regretful thoughts to an end.

'Forensics here. Re Donaldson. Confirming the obvious, there was no forced entry, although the outside light had evidently been recently broken. Our guesstimate is the intruder used his shoulder to slam open the door once it was unlocked and had begun to be opened. Because his shoulder would have moved as the door gave way, the very faint smudge imprints are of use solely to estimate height.

'The probable sequence of events is provided by marks on the stairs and the hall floor. After Donaldson had been coshed to the ground, the dog came down the stairs to attack the intruder, was killed. There was no evidence in the dog's mouth to suggest it gained a hold.

'Donaldson died where he lay. With one exception, all the blood on him was his own. That exception was on the cuff of the jacket. This came from the dog, not the intruder. Probably, having killed it, he went over to Donaldson to check there was no life left and the dog's blood dripped from the cosh.

'We checked Drury's clothes, with a view to linking the two cases, but came up with nothing. If the same villain attacked both men, he left behind no evidence to prove it.

'You already know that there were no meaningful dabs. So I'm afraid we've nothing of real significance to offer. When will the PM be?'

'Tomorrow.'

'I suppose there is the chance something useful will turn up.'

'When this case isn't smelling lucky?'

The fax came through the next morning. The man who had imitated a constable on security detail was named Daniel Fitch. When questioned, he had produced an alibi, provided by two witnesses. Although highly suspect, this could not be broken. The CPS had decided there was little chance of his being convicted, so the case was dropped. Information later received was to the effect that the two witnesses to the alibi had been forced to lie by threats; when questioned, both of them denied this, and there was insufficient evidence to prove them liars.

Details of previous convictions, mugshots, and Fitch's criminal record were provided.

*   *   *

The forensic pathologist checked with the scientists and the SOCO officers that they had the external samples they wanted. Many photographs were taken, many more would be. The body was washed, and this revealed there were no further injuries. An internal examination was carried out. Blood was taken from a large vein, samples of urine, stomach contents, liver, and hair were stored in contamination-free plastic containers and handed to the scientists.

The pathologist, who had been giving a running commentary, taped, of what he had done and found, stripped off surgical hat, mouth and nose mask, gown and gloves. He crossed to Carren. 'There's nothing to add. The weapon was almost certainly some form of cosh, probably metallic. It caused very extensive damage to the skull.' He looked at his watch.

'I was hoping for something solid,' Carren said gloomily.

'Don't they say that hope makes for a good breakfast, but a bad supper?'

Constable Park walked into The Duke's Head. One man left, even though he had not finished his drink.

'A half of Gorman's,' Park said to the bartender. While the real ale was being siphoned into a glass, he casually looked around. Seated in one corner, with three other men, was Syd Agross – his canary. He gave no obvious sign of recognition, scratched the lobe of his right ear. Informers led risky lives and care was always taken to prevent their being suspected.

He paid for his drink, spoke to the man who stood to his right. Was Manchester United going to win the championship? He thought so, the other did not. Chelsea was a far better team, he was told.

'I suppose I'd better move,' Park said. 'The old woman will start shouting if I'm late back.'

'Like that?'

'Aren't they all?'

'Too right.'

He wasn't married and had no immediate intention of becoming so. He liked the girls and gained much credit in their eyes when he explained how law and order in Flexford depended on his energy and skills.

He maintained a sharp distinction between work and play, so there was no second half pint of bitter. He left the pub, crossed to his car, settled behind the wheel and waited. Eventually, Agross joined him.

'Still enjoying the luxury of living, then,' Park observed.

Agross was not amused; if it became known he was an informer, he could expect a beating at best, a cut throat at worst.

'There's a fortune for some information, Syd.'

'How big?'

'A tenner.'

'Do I look that skint?'

'Don't push your luck. There's talk you did the Haram job, and I could wonder if that's good talk.'

'It's shit talk. You know that's not my style.'

'I don't mind trying to fit it on you.' He laughed. 'Come on, Syd, relax, that's just a smile. Ten smart ones for telling me if there's a new face around. Couldn't be easier money if you printed it yourself.'

'What's the name?'

'Fitch.'

'Ain't heard it.'

'Then have a look at this.' Park passed across a copy of the police photograph – full and side face.

'Might have seen someone looks like him.'

'An incomer?'

'Yeah.'

'Where from?'

'Up north.'

'What's his handle?'

'Charlie Wate.'

'Well, well! I love you, Syd.'

'Lay off.'

'Purely a momentary rush of satisfaction. Where do I go looking for him?'

'Can't say.'

'Then start finding out.'

'What's his form?'

'Helping old ladies across the road.'

'Is he hard?'

'As soft as goose fat. So when you have news, get on the blower with our unlisted number.'

Two men left the pub and did not immediately walk away. Agross hurriedly looked to his right so that his face was not visible to them. After a while, he asked, 'Have they gone, guv?'

'All clear, as the wife said to the cupboard when her husband drove away.'

Agross left. A man who'd sell his mother to anyone blind enough to buy her, Park thought as he turned the key to start the engine. Before driving off, he mentally confirmed he had entered in the information book his intention to meet an informer before he left divisional HQ. A requirement intended to make it more difficult for a lawyer to claim he was illegally in cahoots with a villain.

The first phone call was made two days later. Ingham answered it.

'Mr Park?'

'Not in sight right now. Would you like to give a message?'

The answer was the dialling tone.

The second call was on the fourth day. Park was in the CID room.

'It's me, mister.'

Park identified the caller immediately. Agross's speech had an unusual rhythm. 'Morning. Trust you're in continuing health.'

'I got it.'

'Then share your knowledge.'

'What about the tenner?'

'Waiting for you as always.'

'Newood Road.'

'Number?'

'Twenty-three.'

The small van, on the sides of which was painted an advertisement for a chocolate drink that brought out the sun on the darkest day, was parked in Newood Road. The two front seats were empty; ostensibly, the van had been left there by a local resident. In the rear, two policemen kept visual watch on No. 23 through a spyhole with a wide-angle lens, concealed in the vivid orange in the advertisement. By the side of the current watcher was an enlarged photograph of Fitch, a large tin in which were sandwiches, a crumpled slice of sponge cake, and two plastic bottles of water.

A car passed and drew into a space further along the road. The driver stepped out on to the pavement, locked the car, and walked towards No. 23.

'Bingo! As large as life and twice as ugly.' The watcher called out the registration number of the car and his companion noted this down.

'Joe's news was good for, once.'

'Then he must have got things muddled. How long do we give it before we move? Half an hour so as our lad doesn't wonder why the van's moved quickly?'

'Until dark.'

'That's bloody hours away.'

'You heard the skipper. We have to find out if he's on his own.'

'If we're cooped up in here much longer, I'll knock on the front door and ask him.'

Carren, seated behind his desk, looked up. 'Yes, Mike?'

It was not often the inspector used Christian names. Frenley wondered what was responsible for this informality. 'The two lads are back from surveillance, sir. They confirm Fitch is at that address. I've had a run on his car's number. It's very recently been registered in the name of Wate.'

'So is the polecat in his lair?'

'How's that?'

'Fitch is another name for a polecat.'

'I see.' He didn't. 'They maintained their watch. Some forty minutes after he went in, a woman turned up and joined him. All home comforts.'

'We need an identification from Drury. Explain what's what and stress how important his evidence is.'

Drury entered divisional HQ, spoke to the sergeant in the front room. 'I've been asked to come here and see Detective Inspector Carren. My name is Drury.'

'Yes, sir. I'll call someone to show you up to his room.' He spoke on the internal phone.

A constable arrived, noted the sergeant's nod, crossed to where Drury waited. 'Evening, sir. Will you come this way?'

They climbed the stairs, walked along a corridor to the conference room. 'The inspector will be with you immediately.'

Drury entered a large, dull room – the single window was insufficient for the space, and the walls had been painted a dark, institutional brown. There was a table, around which were half a dozen chairs, a phone, a blackboard, and a tired print of Sir Robert Peel.

Carren, a ledger in his hand, hurried into the room, followed by Frenley. 'Thanks for coming in so quickly, Mr Drury.'

'I gathered it was important.'

'It is. I'd like you to look through a number of photographs and tell me whether you identify any of them.'

He put the ledger down on the table, opened it at the first page on which, in cardboard frames, were eight photographs of men, viewed full face and half face.

At the sixth page, Drury said, 'I've met him. Went down for six years if I'm remembering correctly.'

'Would you continue looking, please.'

'This is a visual criminal's who's who?'

'One might call it that.'

Since criminals were no longer branded on their cheeks or had their ears cropped, the subjects looked like any other man: one closely resembled his cousin. On the fourth row of the ninth page was a photograph that brought back unwelcome memories. 'He is the man who knocked me over in the car park.'

'What is the number under the photo?'

'Fifty-five.'

Frenley looked at the list of names in his right hand. He nodded.

'Thank you, Mr Drury,' Carren said. 'That's all for the moment, but you will be asked to attend an identity parade in the near future.'

'I've struck lucky?'

'I suppose that depends on whose viewpoint you are considering.'

Drury left. It had been interesting to experience the

proceedings which brought a man to the dock. One prosecuted or defended him according to one's brief.

Drury dialled the hotel and was connected almost immediately.
He asked to speak to Señora Drury.

'Please wait a moment, señor,' the receptionist said, in
well-pronounced English.

After a brief wait, Diana said, 'Steve?'

'Hopefully, you weren't expecting anyone else. How's
Wendy?'

'So fit! It's thrilling to see her.'

'And you?'

'Never mind me. Are you better?'

'Much better.'

'Is that the truth?'

'The truth, the whole truth, and nothing but the truth.'

'No headache?'

'Just the occasional hint of one.'

'I bet it's more than that. I'll regret bringing Wendy back
to the cold and rain, but I can't wait to return and make
certain you really aren't badly injured.'

'Audrey's looking after me like an old-fashioned matron.
I forgot I had to go back for yet another check-up at the
hospital, and she gave me hell for not reminding her. All but
threw me into her car, and when one of the staff complained
about my missing the appointment, she took care to point
out that hospitals were there for the sake of patients, not the
other way around.'

'Very Audreyish. What did they say about you?'

'I am making a full recovery, so I'm hoping to return to
work soon.'

'For heaven's sake, it's only just over a week since you
were attacked.'

'A man must do what a man must do. If I don't, Alec Rice
will have to pass on all the briefs that are no doubt flooding
into chambers with my name on them.'

'You sound cheerful.'

'I've reason to be, apart from missing Wendy and you.'

'Look, if you're not up to meeting us at the airport . . .?'

'I would drive to John O'Groats to collect you.'

'That wouldn't be very helpful, since we're arriving at Gatwick.'

Minutes later, he went through to the sitting room where Audrey and her husband were watching television.

'You've phoned her?' Audrey asked challengingly.

'I have, and she says it's thrilling to see how fit Wendy is.'

'Calls for a drink,' Timpson said as he stood.

'Is there anything that doesn't, as far as you're concerned?' she asked.

'An invitation to a TT luncheon.'

'They said on the telly yesterday that one small gin and tonic and one small glass of wine each day is all that a person should drink.'

'Before one reaches fifteen.'

Drury admired his brother-in-law for the way in which, with light amusement, he countered Audrey's attempts to control his life.

Jane returned to the sitting room, did not sit. 'Your meal's ready. It needs heating, so I've put it in the microwave. Give it five minutes.'

'What are you having?' Ingham asked.

'I'm not hungry and I'm tired, so I'm going up to bed.'

'I feel like I've been on duty for the past few days, so I'll be with you as soon as I've eaten.'

'No need to rush. I'm sleeping in the spare room.'

'You . . . you're what?'

'It's sad to see that surprises you.' She left.

SEVEN

'If you think you can identify someone in the line-up, Mr Drury, will you please give the number he is holding and say nothing more.'

The constable's words were being taped so that no lawyer should have the chance to allege that, if an identification was made, Drury had been primed as to whom to name. A lawyer would, of course, still try to make such claim.

Lights were switched on and ten men, their numbered cards held up, became sharply visible. Through the one-way glass, Drury studied them. Each wore a hat with brim pulled well down and a raincoat with collar turned up.

'Could they turn to their right so I can see them in profile?'

The order was given. They turned.

'And to the left.'

They turned again.

'Number eight,' Drury said.

'You are satisfied your identification is a true one?'

'Yes.'

The lights were dimmed and the ten men filed out.

'Thank you for your help,' Carren said.

Drury left, not knowing the name of the man he had identified.

'Tell Ingham to question him,' Carren said.

Frenley's surprise was clear. 'I thought you'd be doing that, sir.'

'Next time.'

'But . . . Like I said, Joe's not at his sharpest right now.'

'So if he's more interested in his own troubles than in Fitch's, it'll show. And since I don't want Fitch clamming up before he has to admit who he is, there's hope it'll seem to him to be no more than a trawling visit.'

Ingham parked on the opposite side of the road to No. 23,

Newood Road, a terraced house. He did not hurry to get out of the car, looked at his watch. Jane would probably just have finished her ration of one bun and one cup of tea. That was, if she was still at home. Very emotional, his unfounded, illogical, clumsy suspicion had caused her so much distress, she might have decided to leave home and seek support from her mother or the closest of her friends. Home would no longer be home. Someone had written that a coward died many times before his death; a guilty imagination could be crueller.

He finally crossed the road, knocked on the front door of No. 23. It was opened by a woman who would not have looked out of place in the red-light district of the town; badly waved blonde hair with dark roots, a face heavily made-up, and a dress with a low neckline and high hem-line. 'Is Mr Wate in?'

'Why d'you want to know?' she demanded, her speech coarse.

'I'd like to talk to him.'

'You're fuzz, ain't you?'

'County CID.'

Her automatic dislike was mixed with contempt for his dull manner, as Carren had hoped. 'He ain't here.'

'Where is he?'

'Wouldn't know.'

'Who are you?'

'Cinderella.'

A door slammed open inside the house and there was a call from the far end of the narrow, dark passage. 'Who the sod is it?' a man called out.

'He's my brother,' she said hastily to Ingham. They both heard him advance. Her voice rose. 'It's the fuzz.'

'Wouldn't reckon from the look of him that he was smart.' He came to a stop, faced Ingham. 'What d'you want?'

'A chat.'

'Got a warrant?'

'No.'

'Then bugger off.'

'I need to ask a few questions.'

'Why?'

'Sorting things out.'

'Nothing to sort out.'

'It's easier done here than down at the station.'

He returned to the room from which he had come. Accepting this as permission to enter, Ingham stepped inside.

The woman slammed the door shut behind him.

'I still haven't learned your name?' he said to her.

'Because I ain't said it.'

'There's reason for me not knowing?'

'Daisy Allen,' she said angrily.

The front room had the appearance of a couple of mornings after. Empty tins were on the worn carpet, cigarette butts littered the tiled surface in front of the electric fire, and plates with dirty cutlery and the remains of meals were on a table.

Fitch, now seated, looked at Daisy and indicated the door with a nod. She left. Ingham sat on the settee, hastily moved to escape an obtrusive spring. 'Is your name Charlie Wate?'

'It ain't Gordon Brown.'

'Have you lived in Devil's Hillside?'

'No.' Contempt was replaced by caution.

'It's a strange sort of name. Did the natives believe the devil lived there?'

There was no answer.

'The police up there have asked us to check on who you are.'

'Never leave a man alone, any of you.'

'Sounds as if you have a record.'

He cursed himself for his giveaway comment.

'Is your true name Daniel Fitch?'

'Wate. W-A-T-E.'

'Odd! Still, I've a mobile print-outfit in the car, so I'll take yours and prove them wrong.'

'You ain't taking nothing.'

'When it'll clear up the misidentification?'

Fitch stood, walked over to the cluttered mantelpiece, drew a cigarette out of a pack and lit it.

'You'll know we can gain authority to force you to give your prints.'

He dropped the barely smoked cigarette on to the hearth.

'You're Daniel Fitch – right? Seems they're keen to have you back at Devil's Hillside. Could be because they want to take you to the top of the hill and offer you up as a sacrifice. Or maybe it's to confirm you were the right villain who often dressed up as a copper in order to eyeball a mark.'

Fitch evidently accepted it would be fruitless to continue to deny his identity. 'That wasn't me.'

'From what we've been told, a local justice of the peace, who'd previously seen you in his court, lived in the last house you went to. You fled the scene, but were later charged with impersonating an officer with the intention of committing theft.'

'I was found innocent.'

'Only of that charge, and it's more accurate to say you were not found guilty. Thanks to two women who swore on oath you were with them at the time. Didn't have much chance to do otherwise, since you'd told them that if they didn't, someone would be along to cut their throats.'

'I ain't ever threatened anyone.'

'Records say you smashed up one of your previous victims.'

'He came at me with a sword.'

'And your claim of self-defence failed because the victim was over eighty and the "sword" was a broom handle.'

'He was lying.'

'How long have you lived in Flexford?'

'A few months.'

'What brought you down here?'

'Wanted to go straight.'

'You couldn't manage to do that up there?'

'They was trying to fit me with the uniform job.'

'Since coming south, you've played it white?'

'On me oath, and if you've any more questions, I ain't bleeding well answering them.'

Fitch left the room.

As Ingham opened the front door, Daisy appeared and stared at him, but said nothing.

Ingham reported to Carren. 'He finally admitted he was Fitch, sir,' he said dully.

Carren wondered if Ingham's wife had taken off with another man. Or, this being the age of choice, another woman. 'Did he ask why he'd been called in to the identity parade?'

'No.'

'Did you mention the Donaldson murder?'

'Kept right away from it.'

'And he did the same?'

'Yes.'

'Good.'

'Sir . . .'

'There's something more?'

'A woman is shacked up with him. Daisy Allen.'

'That's significant?'

'It may seem rather far-fetched . . .' He became silent.

'But relevant, judging by your last suggestion.'

'Up north, he covered himself with an alibi given by two women who were scared of him. What if, like many villains, he reckoned he was on to a winner? So down here, he's fixed up his alibi before he needs it. And Daisy Allen knows what will happen to her if she doesn't back him up.'

'It makes sense.'

Ingham left.

Carren went into the makeshift office of the detective chief superintendent. Moss was on the phone, berating someone whom he was accusing of carelessness. He nodded as an indication to sit.

He finally finish the call. Carren repeated Ingham's evidence and his suggestion.

'That lad may look like life's left him stranded, but his brain is still working. This Daisy Allen will back Fitch all the way?'

'It's probably best to accept so.'

'But Fitch hasn't been asked to provide an alibi?'

'No. And there's been no mention of the Donaldson case. But he must know why we're interested.'

'You want to force the alibi so we can shred it before any trial?'

'I don't see a feasible alternative, sir.'

Moss rested his elbows on the table that was doing duty as a desk. 'Our lad suggests Daisy will provide the alibi to save having her throat cut. So once we know the details of the alibi, we can test them. And persuade her that her best interest lies in confessing the truth about what Fitch was really up to that night so we can make certain her throat remains whole.'

EIGHT

Park checked his hair in the car's rear-view mirror. He would have scorned any suggestion of narcissism, but he liked to be certain he was smart when meeting a woman.

He left the car, walked along to No. 23, knocked on the front door. He'd been told Daisy Allen was a really smart number, a candidate for any catwalk, a woman to make one's thoughts gallop. She opened the door. Humour in the CID room was of barrack-room character.

'Another one,' she said bitterly.

'We're moths around a candle.'

'Bloody daft.'

'Intoxicated by beauty.' He was speaking like a punk Romeo, but she looked like the type of woman who would respond to that. 'By my heart, I have just met the fairest of them all.'

'You lot don't have hearts.'

'If I see a lady needing help, I rush to give it to her.'

'And then clear off to avoid a paternity test.'

'Have you anything on the horizon?'

'What's it to you?'

'I have to ask questions that will take time. I'm hoping you'll be willing – to answer them.'

'Hope yourself silly, and it still won't do you any good.'

To show how eager she was for him to leave, she stepped to one side, which allowed him to enter.

'What are they?' she asked as he shut the door.

'Twin peaks of beautiful harmony.'

'What are the *questions*?'

'Could we sit down while I try to remember?'

'Only if there's half the room between us.'

'Your suspicion smites me.'

'A lot more will get smitten if you try anything.' She went into the front room, walked past the settee to sit on a chair. 'What is it?'

'You're saying it's business before pleasure?'

'There ain't any pleasure for you.'

'I am desolate.'

'You're a randy bastard.'

'D'you want to know why I'm here?'

'You've made it clear what you'd like.'

'There's been complaints. He says you're running a cathouse.'

'Who does?'

'A neighbour. Says men are in and out of here quicker than an underground train station in the rush hour.'

'Who's saying this?'

'No names means no shouting.'

'It's a bloody lie.'

'Ten days ago, in the evening, he took video shots of this house with a digital camera that records date and time. Between nine in the morning and four in the afternoon, five men came in here, and none of 'em stayed more than fifteen minutes. Been working too hard.'

'When's ten days ago?'

He shrugged his shoulders.

She left the room, returned with a calendar that had a large page for each month. 'Ten days ago was Monday the eighth.'

'Could be.'

'I wasn't here. So that makes a bleeding liar of him and his camera.'

'I believe you. But you don't mind me asking where you were? My job is to check and double-check.'

'Me and my partner went to the theatre in London and stayed at a hotel afterwards.'

'You wouldn't have receipts or tickets, though, since you weren't paying.'

'I was.'

'Your companion was twice lucky. A peach of a gorgeous lady providing him with free entertainment.'

'He's been having a rough time.'

'So have I.'

'Hope it gets rougher.'

'Then likely it was you who was given the tickets and receipts. But you won't have kept them. Pity!'

'Why?'

'They'd convince my boss the story of you running a cathouse was the nonsense any respectable person would know it to be.'

'I may have stuffed them into my bag.'

'If you did, find them and give me a glimpse and I can tell the boss he can forget the shameless slander.'

She once again left. When she returned, she handed him the theatre programme and a receipt for a double bedroom on the 8/9th November at the Stonybrooke Hotel.

'Is it all right if I keep these to show his royal highness? I'll bring them back as soon as he's seen them.'

'Chuck 'em.'

'And miss the chance of seeing you again?' He stood.

'You lot called Dan in to the station earlier.'

'Didn't know that. No one ever tells me anything.'

'He likely won't be back for a while.'

'And you only tell me that when I have to leave?'

She was obviously annoyed by the unspoken rejection of her offer. 'You think you'd get anywhere if he was away all day?'

'A man can only hope.'

The theatre manager was asked to question his staff to determine whether on Monday, the eighth, a theatre-goer had paid for two tickets, yet only one of the seats had been occupied during the evening performance. He replied it had not been a full house that night and the staff would have had no way of knowing which of the empty seats had been paid for, and which hadn't.

The assistant manager of the Stonybrooke Hotel said it was not the hotel's custom to enquire into the occupancy of rooms. However, at the request of the police, the staff had been questioned. All the chambermaid could say was that, as far as she could remember, the double bed had shown signs of being slept in by two people.

'Had the intelligence to spend half the night on one side of the bed, half on the other,' Frenley opined.

Moss, in the front passenger-seat of the CID Escort, stared

across the road at No. 23. 'You describe her as a bit of a slag?'

'Yes, sir,' Park replied. 'But amusing.'

'Not certain I recognize the combination.' He opened the door, climbed out of the car and crossed the road, followed by Park.

Daisy Allen opened the front door. She ignored Moss, addressed Park. 'Now bloody what?'

Moss introduced himself. His rank evidently troubled her, and her manner briefly became subdued. They followed her into the front room, sat. She looked from one to the other, and fiddled with a button on her dress. 'What is it this time?' she nervously asked.

'Constable Park has previously spoken to you,' Moss said.

'So?'

'You told him you and Wate, or Fitch as I will now call him, were up in London on the eighth. You went with him to the theatre and spent the night at a hotel.'

'Ain't no law against that.'

'What was the play you saw?'

'*A Promethean Problem.*'

'Did you enjoy it?'

'Not really.'

'What was it about?'

'Never understood.'

'You didn't read the description in the programme?'

'Someone torches a house in which a man who swindled him lives and is trapped in the fire. The bloke who wrote it didn't know his arse from his elbow. Use petrol for a job, you don't throw in a match until you're clear enough not to get roasted.'

'Was it a popular play?'

'The theatre was full.'

'Which is why the usherette noticed there was one seat empty and, because this was the only one, she noticed and can describe you.'

'There weren't no empty seat. Charlie was with me.'

'Not according to her.'

'Must have been when he went out for a leak.'

'Do you understand that, whatever he calls himself now, Fitch is in serious trouble?'

She didn't answer.

'And to try to save himself, will ask you to lie. If there's a court case, you will be called to provide him with the false alibi you've just given.'

'I ain't lying.'

'Perjury is a serious offence and heavily punished.'

The fiddling with the button increased.

'Has he threatened you, if you don't lie and swear he was with you on that date at that time?'

'Course he ain't.'

'It happens from time to time, and we can make certain that threat is never carried out. The witness is guarded and, where necessary, provided with a new home, new identity, and the certainty that she will never be traced. You will enjoy that freedom if you admit the truth.'

'I've told it.'

Moss stood. 'When you change your mind, get in touch.'

'As likely as me joining you in the peg house.'

They left, settled in the car. Moss said, 'Peg house is not an expression I have come across before. No doubt you can tell me what it means?'

'A male brothel, sir.'

'I am surprised you said you found her amusing.'

In Interview Room 2, Carren and Frenley sat on one side of the table, Fitch and his solicitor, Vickery, on the other. The tape recorder had been primed with date, time, place, and names of those present.

'Thank you for coming,' Carren said pleasantly.

'Didn't have much option—' Fitch began.

'My client is happy to assist the law in any way he can,' Vickery said. He was smoothly handsome, dressed in a bespoke suit, drove a Mercedes, lived in a manor house, and owned a second property near Florence. As he was fond of saying, the wages of sin are plentiful. He was respected as a solicitor, disliked as a person.

Carren addressed Fitch, his tone easy. 'We're investigating the death of Mr Peter Donaldson and believe you may be able to help us.'

'Don't know nothing about it.'

'I will start by establishing certain facts. Your name is,
contrary to the one you have been using, Daniel Fitch. You
have lived up north in a town called Devil's . . .' He broke
off and spoke in a low voice to Frenley. 'Devil's Hillside?
Is that correct?'

'Yes.'

'While there, you have in the past been found guilty of
several offences.'

'I'm going straight now.'

'At your last appearance in court, it was alleged you had
visited a house dressed as a police constable and claiming
to be advising on security matters?'

'Wasn't me. They couldn't prove nothing.'

'My client,' Vickery said, 'was tried on indictment and
found not guilty after proving his innocence with an alibi.'

'An alibi provided by two female friends?'

'Yes,' Fitch muttered.

'Did they provide your alibi willingly?'

'Of course they did.'

'Inspector Carren,' Vickery said, 'this question was raised
in court, and it was held that the alibi had been given truthfully and voluntarily.'

'Mr Fitch, ten days ago, late in the evening, a man gained
entrance into Abbey Building, the house and business place
of Mr Donaldson. The evidence makes it obvious that he did
not force the entry. Yet it was so late, Mr Donaldson was so
conscious of security, it was very difficult to understand why
he should have admitted the caller. Particularly as the outside
light had, it appears, recently been smashed. Have you any
suggestion as to why he did?'

'My client is under no obligation to answer,' Vickery said
before Fitch could speak.

'Nevertheless, in view of your client's claim that he knows
nothing concerning the tragic death of Mr Donaldson, and
in view of his experience, it's difficult to understand why he
would not have a theory.'

'Maybe he—' Fitch began.

'Leave them to theorize,' Vickery said hastily.

'You were, perhaps, about to surmise that a friend had
called?' Carren said. 'That is most unlikely. We remained

perplexed until we read an article in a certain local newspaper.'

'What paper?' Vickery asked.

'The *Drigg Gazette*.'

'You have a copy of the article?'

'Yes.'

'I should like to read it.'

Carren passed a photocopy across the table. 'Following the facts detailed, we considered the possibility a similar method of gaining unopposed entry might have been employed at Mr Donaldson's home. That led us to ask the northern force to send us information concerning the relevant details of the trial.'

'My client was found not guilty.'

'Indeed, but the photograph of your client, taken because he had been found guilty of previous offences, was sent to us. This photo was shown to the victim of an attack that occurred shortly after the alarm had sounded at Mr Donaldson's home, and he identified your client as his attacker.'

'It seems you had persuaded yourself of my client's guilt before he voluntarily came here at your request. Are you accusing him of the murder of Mr Donaldson?'

'I am about to arrest him on such charge.'

NINE

A file was prepared for the Crown Prosecution Service. This included all statements taken by the police, irrespective of whether they were helpful or unhelpful to the prosecution. All relevant information not intended to be part of the prosecution's case was made available to the defence. As was laid down by law, although the defence did not have to inform the prosecution what their case would be, they did have to give details of any alibi to be offered.

A report from the CPS, some time later, noted that the lack of firm evidence needed to refute the alibi made any challenge to it likely to be of dubious success. However, in their opinion, it was in the interests of the public, to prosecute.

Except for the large coat of arms on the wall behind the bench, there was no colour in the courtroom. Without wigs and gowns being worn by the magistrates or by any barrister appearing in court, there was nothing visually to remind one of the long age of neutral justice that the country had enjoyed. Few public bothered to attend the daily routine of minor thefts, drunk and disorderlies, vandalisms, and so on, but the committal proceedings in a case of murder attracted many, even if the morbid interest in seeing someone threatened with death by hanging had long since been lost.

Drury was called to the witness box and took the oath. He gave his name, address and occupation. Counsel – a barrister, since this was a major crime – stood. 'Mr Drury, will you describe to the court what happened on your return from an evening spent with friends who live in this town?'

'I was late leaving them because it had been an amusing evening . . .'

The questioning continued. Seventy minutes after Drury had begun his evidence, counsel sat. Defence had chosen to be represented by Vickery.

'Mr Drury, you have told the court the time was between

one thirty and two in the morning when you were knocked
down by a man as you were entering the small parking square
at the back of the supermarket. Did you hear him approach?'

'I wasn't consciously aware of doing so.'

'Then you did not turn round to see who it was?'

'No.'

'The square is a private parking space, owned by the supermarket. Did you have permission to park in it?'

'No.'

Vickery looked at the bench. Here was a man, he wished
them to understand, who did not respect private property.
'Will you describe the lighting in the square?'

'There is no light in it. Beyond is a street lamp, the
luminosity of which reaches over the wall.'

'Would you describe the square as well lit?'

'No.'

'Can you be more precise? Would you judge that inside
the square at night, one would be able to read a newspaper?'

'Only with some difficulty.'

'Was yours the only car in the square when you returned?'

'There was one other present.'

'What make was it?'

'I did not notice.'

'Could you judge whether it was a saloon, a hatchback,
or an estate?'

'There wasn't time. I only noted it for a second before I
was bowled over.'

'After you were knocked to the ground, you were struck
over the head by a weapon of some sort. Did you lose
consciousness?'

'Yes, for a very brief moment.'

'When you recovered consciousness, you were, at the very
least, confused?'

'Yes.'

'You told the police your assailant was wearing a hat pulled
well down over the head and a raincoat with the collar turned
up. Then, even in daylight, much of his face would have
been obscured?'

'Possibly.'

'If the man was walking away from you as you lay on the

ground, it seems logical to assume you had no chance to see his face.'

'That's correct.'

'What did the man do after you were knocked down?'

'He crossed to the other car and opened the driving door. That resulted in the interior light going on.'

'With what effect?'

'I was able to see his face.'

'You told the police that despite the confusion in your mind, and the fact you were lying on the ground and therefore your line of sight was greatly reduced, you saw his face sufficiently clearly to be able to identify him?'

'Yes.'

'Were you asked to identify him from a photograph?'

'Yes.'

'Did you do so?'

'Yes.'

'Did you name anyone as your assailant at an identity parade?'

'I gave the number of the man I recognized.'

'Whom did you identify?'

'The accused.'

Vickery sat.

Drury was one of the few in court who was not surprised that Vickery did not conduct a longer and sharper cross-examination. But those others failed to understand that Vickery, having decided there was no chance of avoiding committal, accepted it was in the defendant's interest to raise points in his favour, but not to pursue them until the trial.

Fitch was committed. Bail was refused.

TEN

Drury returned to the flat a few minutes before six.
'How did it go?' Audrey asked as she came out of the sitting room.

'Much as expected.' He dropped his overcoat on to the hall chair.

'Would it be too difficult to hang that up in your room?'

'Yes, sweet sister, it would, as I'm driving home in a minute to check how things are there.'

'Don't be ridiculous. You're not fit enough to drive that far.'

'Six miles is not exactly a Le Mans.'

'It's dark.'

'Hopefully, the headlights will work.'

'Mother always said you were as stubborn as a mule.'

'Did she? . . . Tomorrow is her birthday.'

'Nine years. But I still find myself wanting to tell her or ask her something every now and then. People do survive death, in memories.'

Timpson stepped into the hall. 'Deep philosophical thoughts?'

'Which you won't understand.'

'Since the nature of being as opposed to the act of being has never interested me, don't bother to try to enlighten me. Come on in, Steve.'

'Sorry, but I have to leave.'

'You do not! You're just being pig-headed,' she said sharply.

'I'm glad I don't have a sister!' Timpson laughed.

Parkside Farm, a large, timber-framed cottage, built in the latter part of the seventeenth century, was confusingly named, since it bordered woodland, not parkland. A small orchard of Granny Smith apple trees separated the smaller garden and house from the road. To the back was the larger garden and beyond, a field and the woods.

Drury braked to a halt, switched off the engine and lights, picked out a torch from a side pocket in the driving door, and left the car. The air was cold, but fresh; from the woods came the eerie sound of a vixen's call. He switched on the torch and walked past the garage to the garden gate, which he had been promising himself to repaint for ages, yet had never found the time to do so. A sweep of torchlight showed the garden to be in good condition. The retired milkman who looked after the flowerbeds, lawn, and the cobnut bushes and trees took as much pride in his work as if the garden were his.

Drury rounded the corner of the house, continued along the brick path to the front door. The hall light, controlled by a time switch – as were the other main lights – was on. He unlocked the door, stepped inside, and once more enjoyed the solid beauty of the beamed hall. Diana loved the house as much as he did, and Wendy was beginning to appreciate its qualities, even when compared to the large, modern, soulless house, but with indoor swimming pool, of one of her particular friends.

The phone rang, startling him. Audrey, determined to make certain he did not stay too long? He crossed to the corner cupboard, lifted the receiver, and gave their phone number, as was his custom.

'I've finally got through to you.'

The female voice was not one he recognised.

'I've been ringing and ringing.'

She sounded as if he was to blame. 'I'm sorry about that,' he said formally.

'Georgina Smith speaking. Will you put me through to Diana?'

Was 'please' an unknown word? 'She's not here.'

'I want to speak to her.'

Why else would this woman be phoning? 'She's abroad. Wendy's been suffering badly from asthma, and we were advised to take her somewhere sunny to see if that would help.'

'Have they gone to South Africa?'

'No.'

'Australia? Canada?'

She did not realize that one did not willingly go paddling at this time of the year in Canada? 'Mallorca.'

'Which part?'

Her manner had annoyed him sufficiently to make him say, 'I'm not certain.'

'When will she be back?'

'I've no idea.'

'I'm ringing because we were at school together, and I'm trying to organize a get-together for our year. You can give me the number of her hotel.'

'I haven't got it here.'

'I'll phone again.'

She did not bother to say goodbye. He replaced the receiver, puzzled by the call. Not by her rudeness – that had become quite usual in the name of equality, he sometimes thought – but by her voice. Caring little for political correctness, he would have termed it as uneducated. Yet Diana had gone to public school, and any girl with such an accent would have been taught to change it.

He went into the kitchen. Their Daily-Two – as Diana informally called her – had made certain it was clean and that everything was in its place. He filled the filter machine with water and coffee, switched it on, and then forgetfully crossed to the refrigerator and found it empty. In the larder was a tin of evaporated milk, and it was a case of use that or drink black coffee.

He sorted through the mail, which had been put on the dining-room table. There was nothing of consequence. He went into the hall and dialled the hotel (whose name and number he had said he did not know). There was a time before Diana said, 'Sorry to keep you waiting, love, but we've only just got back from the beach. Had quite a struggle to persuade Wendy to leave since it was becoming quite cool; she wanted to stay until the sun disappeared behind the mountains.'

'She's still full of beans, then?'

'Overflowing. How are things with you?'

'I had to spend most of the day at the magistrates' court as a witness and had to lunch at the nearby café.'

'Not up to the standards of your gourmet tongue? Poor dear! For the first meal on our return, I'll cook duck á l'orange and make a chocolate mousse.'

'That is a contract with no escape clause.'

'I think it'll have to be soon. Wendy's missing school, and I'm missing you.'

'Try to hang on a little longer. Make certain Wendy is tucking into tomatoes, vegetables, and fish, all garnished with olive oil.'

'Fish and olive oil?'

'Enjoy the Mediterranean diet and live to be a hundred!'

'Not always to be desired. She's complaining about missing her favourite foods.'

'Probably mush.'

'She does not eat mush.'

'By the way, an old school friend of yours rang and wanted a word with you. She sounded rather odd.'

'Doris Gethin? She was very odd. She actually liked boiled onions and maths.'

'No, Georgina Smith.'

'Who?'

He repeated the name.

'She wasn't at school with me.'

'Must have been from the way she talked: where were you, what part of the island were you staying in, what was the name of your hotel, what was its phone number?'

'You must have got her name wrong. We had no Georgina, only one Dorothea. The rest of us were plain Jills, Joans, Marys, and Dianas.'

'One Diana was far from ordinary.'

'Am I being big-headed to say, "What gallantry!"?'

Ingham stepped into Moss's 'office'. 'You wanted me, sir?'

'A word before I leave.' Moss struggled to wedge the last file into his briefcase, before giving up and putting it in the suitcase on top of gaily coloured pyjamas. He straightened up. 'I wanted to congratulate you on your imaginative approach to this case.'

'Thank you, sir.'

'Keep it up.' He watched Ingham leave. If it was true he was troubled by domestic problems, he wasn't the first. Women could be angels, but marriage could become the devil.

He picked up the briefcase as Carren came into the room.

'You car's here, sir.'

'Thanks.' He put the briefcase down, sat on the edge of the table. 'You'll do your damndest to break the alibi?'

'Of course, sir, but—'

'She finds the threat of violence more reliable than our offer of protection if she tells the truth.'

'Not surprising, I suppose.'

'Your big problem in achieving a guilty verdict will be that previous convictions are not normally allowed in court, and this will leave you unable to show the sequence of events.'

'Fitch was found not guilty of imitating a police constable in order to commit crime.'

'So will that make the facts permissible? Not a question I can answer off-hand. However, if necessary, prosecuting counsel should find a way of introducing them surreptitiously, if necessary. That's why they're paid . . . How firm is Drury's evidence?'

'He made a good witness at the hearing.'

'Time will tell if he can overcome the obvious suggestion from the defence that the square was so dark he couldn't see his hand in front of his face, and that even if he could have he'd have been too brain-scrambled to recognize it.'

'I think he'll cope, sir. And his initial identification of Fitch will be strengthened by his both picking out the mugshot of Fitch and naming him at the identity parade.'

'Solid evidence that Fitch had been in Donaldson's place would have been a sight better. But if we always had enough evidence to prove the guilty are guilty, we'd become a low crime-rate society.' He slid off the table, picked up his briefcase.

'I'll take the suitcase, sir.'

'Thanks, but I like to think I'm not yet in my dotage. By the way, as I've told him, I like the form of Ingham.'

Ingham poured a whisky, made his way into the sitting room. He remained standing as he stared at the framed photograph of Jane on top of the small bookcase, placed there by him despite her objection that it looked like self-appreciation.

As PR to the managing director of a large firm with interests in the Midlands as well as the South, she frequently had to travel with Sir Richard Cullingham to Birmingham. There, they stayed at the Grand, providing her with a taste of luxury she would not otherwise have enjoyed. She was there now. After he'd finished his drink, he'd phone her. In his mind, an internal conversation began . . . 'It's me, darling. I had to tell you, I've just had a shot in the arm.'

'Less lethal than one in the heart, I suppose.'

Her sense of fun had returned, at least in part. 'I wish I could explain.'

'So do I.'

'We'd been having rather a lot of arguments over my work.'

'You were surprised?'

'Of course not; well, not really. But I had to cancel our theatre treat, and after that . . . You'd gone at me for having left you without any sort of a social life, and I became scared I was going to lose you. So when Alan Bradbury said what he did . . . I was crazy with worry, or I would never have even *begun* to think there could possibly be anything between you and . . . Please, darling. Please forgive me.'

'Steve, I'm sorry I've been so horrible to you, but it hurt so terribly I . . . I think I became a little crazy as well. So let's forget what we said to each other; it just never happened.'

'Darling, the chief superintendent called me in to say he was impressed by my work. He also said so to the guv'nor.'

'Isn't that a feather in your cap?'

'A peacock's tail feather.'

'I'll hurry home so we can celebrate.'

The 'conversation' ceased. For the first time in days, the cloud which had enveloped his mind lifted slightly.

He picked up the mobile, checked the number he wanted, dialled it.

'Grand Hotel. May I help you?' The receptionist spoke in cut-crystal tones.

'I'd like to speak to Mrs Ingham.'

'Your name is?'

He gave it, waited. Emotionally, it was like lying under a descending, swinging pendulum with a sharpened blade. But it was going to rise.

'I'm sorry, Mrs Ingham is not booked into the hotel.'

Jane had remarked more than once that Sir Richard's life ran like a metronome. In Birmingham, he always stayed at the Grand, always dined at nine, and always asked Jane to eat with him. Ingham looked at his watch. 'My wife will be in the dining saloon right now.'

'I'm sorry, but Mrs Ingham is not staying in this hotel.'

'She must be.'

'She is not here, Mr Ingham.' Annoyance sharpened her voice.

He muttered a brief thanks, switched off the mobile, picked up his empty glass and went through to the small larder where he poured himself another and stronger whisky. Had the metronome faltered? Had they had an accident . . .? But they had not even been booked in. Had she been lying?

He had drunk a small cupful of Benbury hot chocolate – for once an advertisement held some veracity; it did help sleep – when the phone in the hall rang. He answered it.

'We've just arrived at the Grand, and the receptionist says you've been trying to get in touch.'

'I rang—'

'To find out if I was here?'

'No, of course not!'

'The receptionist says that when she told you I wasn't, you became very annoyed.'

'Because I thought—'

'That I wasn't here because I'd said I would be? The answer couldn't be anything as simple as a sudden emergency, which meant plans had to be changed. No, I *must* be having an affair with Sir Richard and didn't want you to gain any hint of that. It doesn't matter that he's nearly eighty, married with a grown-up family, is what used to be called a "gentleman", and has always treated me with great respect. He must be screwing me because Reg wasn't available.'

'I couldn't imagine such a terrible thing.'

'Your imagination spends its time in the gutter. When I return, I'll stay with my sister until I decide what to do next.'

The line went dead.

ELEVEN

Drury, in the sitting room, heard Audrey hurry along the corridor to answer the hall phone. A moment later, she looked into the room. 'It's for you,' she said.

'Diana?'

'A man who didn't give his name and who sounded as if he's one of your more unsavoury customers.'

'A barrister has clients; he does not see them unless they are with their solicitors.'

'Have you any more pedantic information?'

'Not until your next solecism.'

'You should wear your wig when you become pompous.'

He laughed, put down the newspaper, and went into the hall. 'Drury here.'

'You keep your gob shut.'

'What . . . Who are you?'

'The bloke what cuts out your sodding tongue if you don't keep quiet.'

The call ended.

'That was not a very prolonged conversation,' Audrey observed curiously when he returned to the sitting room.

'I was told never to talk to strangers.'

'Then he wasn't one of your customers? Sorry, clients.'

'I've no idea who he was.'

'What did he want?'

'My memory to go on holiday.'

'What d'you mean?'

'I'm to forget my evidence in the Donaldson case or I'll have my tongue cut out as a start to proceedings.'

'My God! He was threatening you?'

'A reasonable description.'

'It . . . That's impossible!'

'I'm a very long way from being the first witness for the prosecution to have it suggested I forget what I saw. And it's not all that difficult in court to imply that since one has

always believed truth is the shining sword of justice, one is
forced to admit that one's evidence is not as incontrovert-
ible as first claimed.'

'Don't people go to the police?'

'Some may, but it's a question of balance. The lie in court,
or a painful death out of court?'

'Then guilty people go free?'

'Happens. The tangled laws of evidence contrive to be
always in their favour.'

'What are you going to do?'

'Inform the police, of course.'

'Then . . .'

'Yes?'

'I hope to God your shining sword is strong enough.'

At divisional HQ, the duty sergeant behind the desk in the
front room said, 'Inspector Carren isn't here at the moment,
Mr Drury. Would you like to have a word with Sergeant
Frenley?'

'Yes, I should.'

'If you'd wait over there.' He pointed to the small alcove
containing two chairs and a table, on which was a stack of
out-of-date magazines.

The wait was short. Frenley, looking tired, one eye blood-
shot from rubbing at an irritation, came up to the alcove and
greeted Drury. 'Would you like to come this way?'

Interview room No. 1 was, for no immediately apparent
reason, less oppressive in character than the others. To mark
the difference from a chat and an official interrogation,
Frenley ostensibly checked the recording unit was not turned
on. 'You have some information?' he prompted.

'I had a phone call a couple of days ago,' Drury said. 'A
Georgina Smith wanted to speak to my wife. She claimed
she had been at school with Diana and was trying to arrange
an old-girls' reunion.'

Frenley, perplexed by the seeming irrelevance of what he
was being told, nodded to indicate his attention.

'The Smith woman seemed to know my wife quite well,
yet Diana was positive not only that there had not been a
Georgina Smith in her year, but also that there was no one

of that name in the school. At the time, I decided it was
either a complete mix-up by the other woman, or Diana's
memory was at fault.

'Half an hour ago, I received another unusual phone call,
and I'm wondering if the two are connected. This was from
a man with a very rough voice. I was to forget my evidence,
he said, or my tongue would be cut out as an hors d'oeuvre.'

Frenley, his perplexity gone, said, 'Did he indicate he was
referring to the Donaldson case?'

'No.'

'Did he mention Fitch's name?'

'No.'

'Did you record the number of either caller?'

'I didn't have the sense to look.'

'Where were you?'

'I'd nipped home to make certain all was well and the
first call came through there. She had phoned my sister more
than once, wanting to speak to me, and in the end Audrey
suggested she try my place. The second call came through
to my sister's home.'

'During the first call, when the woman learned your wife
was not there, did she want to know where she was?'

'Yes.'

'Did you tell her?'

'I said Diana was in Mallorca. Then I was asked where,
in what hotel, and what was her telephone number. I was
rather annoyed by all her prying questions and the manner
in which she'd asked them and so said I didn't know.'

'Then all she can be certain is that your wife and daughter
are on the island?'

'Yes.'

'When do you expect them to return?'

'Wendy shouldn't miss any more school, and Diana naturally wants to return home, so it won't be long, although there's
only a provisional date.'

Frenley interlocked his fingers, revolved his thumbs about
each other. 'I have to ask you this. Is it possible a friend is
having a joke at your expense?'

'Quite impossible.'

'Inspector Carren will want to talk to you. In the meantime,

I think it is essential you ask your wife to stay on the island, and also to refuse to tell anyone where she's staying. Whoever is behind this may well judge you unlikely to give into the straightforward threat to yourself, so your family may be seen as potentially another and stronger lever with which to make you recant your identification of Fitch.'

After a moment, Drury said, 'It must sound stupid, but I've been seeing this as an attempt to rig the law, not as a serious threat to my family.'

'Hardly surprising in the circumstances. A threat has the effect of causing a degree of confusion. Another thing. I expect there will be further threats; they usually continue until the objective is either achieved, or clearly won't be. Would you ask your sister not to tell anyone where your wife is staying, to answer the telephone only on the landline, and if her phone has caller identification, to note the number of any caller she does not know personally?'

'Surely, whoever makes a threat by phone will make certain that their number shows as "withheld"?'

'If the caller remembers to do so. But, as you will have learned from your work, most criminals lack sharp intelligence.'

'Unless they're in banking.'

Frenley smiled. 'Good to see you're taking this in your stride, Mr Drury.'

'Nothing else I can do since at the trial, I'll have to repeat the evidence I gave at committal proceedings.'

When Drury returned to Broadway Manor, Audrey and her husband were in the sitting room. He answered her unasked question. 'It's possible Diana and Wendy would be used to make me change my evidence, so I'm to tell Diana they must stay on the island, completely incognito, until this gets cleared up.'

'Bloody swine!' Timpson seldom swore, yet the anger with which he had spoken would have matched four-letter words.

'May I phone Diana again?'

'Why ask?' Audrey demanded.

He looked at his watch and his troubled mind left him unable immediately to remember the difference in times. 'Are we one hour ahead or behind?'

'Behind,' Timpson answered.

'She'll be asleep. It will be somewhat alarming to be woken up to learn what's what. Would it be better to wait until the morning?'

'No,' Audrey said sharply.

He went into the hall, dialled the hotel's number. A man answered in Spanish.

'Señora Drury, please.'

The man switched to English. 'You wish the señora? Here, is late.'

'It's very important.'

'Kindly pause, señor.'

The ringing continued for a while before the sleep-clouded Diana said, 'Who is it?'

'Steve. Sorry to ring at this hour . . .'

'What's happened? Are you in hospital again?'

'I'm perfectly fit, darling, but there is a spot of trouble. Someone is trying to make me change my evidence in the murder case, and there's the possibility that if I refuse to do that, they'll try to put pressure on me by threatening you and Wendy. Since they can't do anything when they don't know where you are, you must stay on the island until the problem's sorted.'

'No! If you're in trouble . . .'

'It will only be trouble if you return.'

'I can't leave you on your own!'

'Neither of us wants this, but better that than my knowing you two are threatened if I don't do as demanded.'

'They . . . they would hurt Wendy?'

'Probably.'

'Christ!'

'Don't get in touch with anyone, don't write to friends, and you must be all right. I'll ring when I can be certain it's safe to do so, otherwise we cut all communication between us. Please understand, there's no other choice.'

'All right,' she muttered.

He was convinced that as she spoke she had been looking at Wendy asleep in the second bed in the room.

Seated in Carren's room, Frenley said, 'Mr Drury arrived and asked to speak to you. Since you weren't here, I had a word with him. When he was not in his sister's flat, there were calls from a Georgina Smith who wanted to speak to him. He'd gone to his home to make certain all was well there, so his sister gave the woman that phone number. Georgina got in touch at Parkside and claimed she was a friend of Drury's wife – they had been at school together and she was organizing a get-together of their class – and wanted to get in touch with Mrs Drury. She became very inquisitive about where Mrs Drury was staying, so much so that in the end he told her he didn't know. When he spoke to his wife later, she was certain there had been no Georgina Smith at the school. Last night, a man – judging by his voice, a rough character – phoned Drury at his sister's. The conversation was brief. If he remembered what he saw, he was told, he'd have his tongue cut out.'

'Shit!' was Carren's immediate comment.

'No direct mention of Fitch, but there obviously didn't have to be. No explanation of why Drury would regret giving honest evidence, but his wife and kid had to be the potential targets.'

'What did you say to him?'

'Make certain they remain in Mallorca, tell no one where they are staying.'

'Then now the intended pressure can't be put on him so successfully. So will he be targeted directly? His evidence needs to be considered vital to a successful prosecution and his elimination would bust that. But his murder would put Fitch slap in the frame.' He drummed on the desk with his fingers, stared out of the window. 'Something's wrong.' He looked back.

'How so, sir?'

'When is the trial expected to be held?'

'Next year, before the end of the Hilary term.'

He stopped drumming. 'So Drury is to be scared into recanting. But a threat is at its most effective when made, not when there's time for the victim to seek help. And Drury, wedded to what lawyers call justice, is ninety-nine per cent certain to report the threat to us. So why threaten now and not much closer to the trial?'

'Perhaps Fitch is too eager to ensure he's found not guilty to realize the danger of making the threat too soon.'

'Suppose Fitch has more intelligence than you're granting him?'

'In that case, I can't see any reason for acting now.'

'Nor can I. Which is the worry.'

There were enough troubles without inventing new ones, Frenley thought.

'Does Drury have a close friend or relative who would provide a target as effective from Fitch's point of view?' Carren asked.

'There is his sister, but apart from her, I don't know.'

'Is Drury scared by the threat?'

'I'd say disturbed, not frightened.'

'Shaken, not stirred,' Carren said, to the surprise of himself as well as Frenley. 'We need to go over everything again.'

'Right, sir, only—'

Carren interrupted him. 'Only it'll be a waste of time?'

TWELVE

'Have you eaten?' Frenley, seated behind his desk, asked Park. A part-time hypochondriac, he wondered if the brief pain in his back was a harbinger of serious trouble.

'Twenty minutes ago, sarge. Shepherd's pie. Made from an old-age-pensioner sheep.'

'You expected steak tartar?'

'Wouldn't have objected.'

'You'll be wanting a bottle of wine with your lunch soon.'

'Wouldn't object to that either.'

'On your bike and have a word with Daisy Allen. Challenge her over the alibi she's offering Fitch.'

'If the DCS didn't get anywhere with her, what hope have I?'

'You're more her type.'

'That's insulting.'

'Surprised you realized that.'

'Sarge, she'll just give the same old story.'

'So you tell her you've proof she's lying.'

'What proof?'

'You're the best liar in the squad, yet I have to explain?'

Daisy opened the front door. 'Bugger off or I'll have you for harassment.'

'You're offering me the chance to harass you?' Park asked.

'Leave me alone. I ain't done anything.'

'Then it's time we started.'

'You think I'd give you a freebie if you was starving?'

'Lighten up, Daisy, and if you'd like to offer me a cup of coffee, I wouldn't say no.'

'*I* will.'

He stepped inside. 'You're looking like a million dollars.'

'And you look like you should've been put down at birth in the name of decency.'

He walked into the sitting room, sat.

'Make yourself at home.'

'Which room upstairs?'

'You've a mind like—'

'You mentioned that last time. Daisy, I like you.'

'It ain't mutual.'

'So I don't want to see you ending up in so much trouble, a fairy godfather couldn't get you out of it.'

'What trouble?'

'Lying to the police, providing a false alibi.'

'I told it straight.'

'Like a barley stick. Remember saying that when you and your pal went to the theatre to see a play called Prom-something-or-other it was full?'

She said nothing.

'Big mistake. The theatre was almost empty.'

'Who says?'

'The manager and the usherettes. And because it was so poorly attended, people were noticed. I described you. Like straight out of the A-list, or something like that. One of the girls remembered you. What about the man she was with, I wondered. On her own, she answered.'

'He was with me.'

'Maybe in spirit, but not in the flesh.'

'I bought two tickets.'

'Which was twice a waste of money. Another thing, d'you remember jogging the waiter's elbow at the restaurant in Stonybrooke Hotel so he had to juggle with the plate he was holding and some gravy splashed on to your hand? Says you swore at him for being clumsy?'

'He's a bleeding liar.'

'You were on your own, but the bottle of wine was empty by the time you finished eating.'

'I was with him,' she said wearily.

'My boss told you what would happen if you went into court and tried to tell a pack of lies. You'd get banged up for years.'

'I'm telling the truth.'

There was a silence.

'Pretty lady, I don't want to think of you in prison with

all those wicked women. And Fitch will go down for so long that when he comes out, he'll have forgotten you and what it's all about. Tell things as they were and you'll have nothing to worry about. Why won't you trust me to say what's best for you?'

'Because I'd sooner trust a rattlesnake.'

'Ronald rang earlier,' Elaine said to Carren, who was settled in their sitting room, a gin and tonic by his side.

He didn't immediately ask how their son and heir was.

'Aren't you interested?'

'Of course I am.' He looked away from the TV. His wife was a normal, sensible person, except where their son was concerned. Ronald's birth had been difficult, his childhood exhausting since he had seldom slept, his schooldays irksome since he was intelligent, yet disinclined to work, and now he was at university, he considered it his parents' duty to fund a champagne lifestyle.

'His tutor complimented him on his project.'

'Makes a change.'

'You're all vinegar. What's the problem – work?'

'Yes.'

'Why can't you leave it behind when you come home?'

'I wish I knew.'

'What's being such a bother?'

'Why does a man who probably isn't a fool act stupidly? Why move before he needed to? Why give an early warning when success calls for delay?'

'I've no idea what you're talking about. Ronald told me he's become really interested in Middle English. He's been studying. "The Legend of Good Women" by Coleridge . . . No, that doesn't sound quite right . . . Perhaps it was Chaucer. The legend was written in an unusual form – something to do with couplets. Ten syllables. Do you understand what that means?'

'There's one less than eleven.'

'I'm sure he'll get a first.'

'How much did you promise to send him?'

'What makes you think I did anything of the sort?'

'History,' he answered.

*   *   *

'I'm sorry,' Moira Young said, 'but Jane has a bad headache and doesn't feel up to coming downstairs to the phone.'

'She has a mobile,' Ingham said. 'I could speak to her on that.'

'It doesn't seem to be working.'

'It won't until she switches it on.'

'Joe, let things ride for a little and I'm sure everything will turn out all right.'

'I wish I could be half as optimistic.'

'She is very upset.'

'I'm not exactly dancing around the moon.'

'Give it time.'

'A lifetime?'

The call finished, he went into the kitchen and poured himself another whisky.

Frenley belched.

'Mike!' Madge said sharply.

'Better out than bubbling.'

'I hope you don't start drinking too much when you're retired.'

'Depends if I'm given the chance.'

'What's up with you this evening? You're as prickly as a hedgehog.'

'Work's being a bastard.'

'Must you talk like that?'

'It helps.'

She was knitting. She knitted sweaters for her husband, for her son, and for charity. 'You are going to *have* to find something to do.'

'The idea of retirement is to stop working.'

'Satan finds mischief for idle hands.'

'He'll have a hard job at my age.'

Drury listened, receiver to his right ear, to his daughter talking. Wendy had met another English girl who lived locally. Her friend said, why didn't she move and go to school there and learn Spanish? Only lessons were in the local language now so she'd have to learn that as well. She could play on the beach, go swimming, and learn to ride with the English lady who had lots and lots of horses. She loved things called *ensaimadas* that were like donuts, but weren't, and one of the waiters at the restaurant was very kind and called her *cariña* which mummy said was nice.

They'd driven into the mountains again, Wendy said, and had lunch at the place where they cooked meat on a fire. It had been scrumptious. She hadn't swum for ages and ages because mummy said the water had become too cold. A man had fallen in the hotel and had been rushed to hospital. The car that had taken him had left with a white handkerchief hanging out of a window to show it was an emergency. Did people do that at home . . .?

When Wendy had stopped talking, Diana took the phone and said, 'You promise nothing's happened?'

'The police are keeping a special watch to make certain it doesn't.'

'Steve, it will be Christmas soon.'

'Already? Tempus fugits ever faster as one ages.'

'We must return home before then.'

'Provided—'

'The weather's changing quickly and it's almost chilly today; someone said the forecast is for a cold, wet winter. Wendy will have gained all the benefit she's going to.'

'The trial won't be until early next year.'

'You expect us to stay here until then, missing Christmas?'

'For safety's sake.'

'You've just said the police are protecting you.'

'Keeping a special watch.'

'And the man's in prison and not on remand?'

'Yes.'

'It'll be safe for us.'

'It can't be until he's in prison on a lifetime sentence.'

'Why?'

'Until he's found guilty of murder, he'll be scheming. All the time he doesn't know where you are, he'll be unable to use you and Wendy to make me alter my evidence.'

'Then . . . Steve, could you come out here?'

'Why not? If I check with the police, and they advise it'll be OK, I will.'

'It's a promise?'

'A conditional one.'

'A positive promise.'

After saying goodbye, he switched off the cordless receiver and replaced it in its holder. Before too long, they could be a family again.

Alec Rice, head clerk of chambers, took more care over his appearance than most, not from any sense of self-esteem, but because he was that kind of a man. Just as his tie was always correctly knotted, his shirt spotless, and his working suit uncreased, so he also made certain the work of chambers was carried out with maximum efficiency. He was known by solicitors as starchy, but very reliable.

Drury climbed the stairs to the open square on the first floor of the pseudo-Georgian building, which had been erected in the middle of the previous century to replace a bombed Victorian one. On the outside door was listed in golden lettering the names of barristers attached to the chambers. He entered. Rice was placing two newly received briefs on the marble mantelpiece above the blocked-up fireplace; each was carefully squared with those already there.

'Good morning, Mr Drury. How pleasant to see you back.' He spoke with the pronunciation and care of a past generation. 'I trust you are fully recovered from the very unfortunate occurrence?'

'Firing on all four cylinders.' Drury automatically read the names on the briefs to make certain whether any of them was for him.

'I have passed on all your work, as you said.'

'Of course.'

'I will ensure your return is known. Mr Hipper will be pleased.'

'A fruitful provider!'

Rice did not consider that an appropriate comment, even if Hipper was known for his mellow voice and studied manners.

The ticket collector – his vinegary visage mocked by his cheerful friendliness – wished Drury good evening and did not bother to look at his season ticket. The walk to the flat was short, but cold; the wind had strengthened, the damp air promised rain. Even if Mallorca had not remained sunny, Wendy would return to very different and unwelcome conditions.

Audrey called out, as he stepped into the flat, 'Steve?'

'In person.' He hung up his mackintosh.

She entered the hall. 'How did it go?'

'Smooth at chambers, rough on the train back. A toad of a man had a long conversation of staggering imbecility on his mobile phone by my right ear.'

'The bane of the twenty-first century. Drown the irritation with a drink. Basil isn't back, so help yourself.'

'I'll wait.'

'Never drink on one's own? I've often wondered why it's presumed that would be fatal when one's much more likely to drink most when in a group. Come on in and get warm.'

He went in. 'I've been thinking.' He sat.

'Am I about to be granted the pleasure of a brilliant exposition?'

'I may go to Mallorca for Christmas.'

'A man of sudden Socratic sagacity!'

'Hullo, Mr Drury.' Carren shook hands.

'I'm sorry to bother you yet again.'

'No problem. Do sit.'

Once seated, Drury said, 'I'd be grateful for some advice.'

'I hope I'll be able to provide it.'

'My wife is very keen for us to have Christmas together. But I told her she mustn't return.'

'Unfortunately, that is so. Should the villains learn she's back here . . . I don't need to flesh out the details.'

'She suggests I go out there instead. I said I would, provided you agreed it couldn't do any harm.'

'I'm not certain I could offer so absolute an assurance.'

'Oh!' Drury's disappointment was immediate.

'In my job, we learn that two and two don't always add up to four; human intervention can make it five. But what I can say is that if precaution is taken, the chances of trouble are light enough to be remembered, but ignored – provided that you tell no one where you are going, and when you are there, you and your family remain very silent.'

'Right.'

'I imagine you will fly?'

'I'm returning to work so I won't be able to afford the time not to.'

'It's best to be thoroughly pessimistic. If known, your absence from here and the proximity to Christmas will lead to the obvious conclusion. They might learn what flight you're booked on – employees are bribeable, e-mails are hackable – and follow you on your journey.'

'You're telling me really it's sensible not to go?'

'No. I'm saying that it will take a little planning to do so with reasonable safety.'

Drury let it be known in the village, at his bank, at chambers, that he was spending Christmas with his cousin in Aberdeen. He flew from Gatwick in the name of Arnold Stevens; his new, digitalized passport confirmed his identity. He arrived at Son Sant Joan Airport, left in a hired car and, as arranged by Carren, was shadowed by *Traffico* until it could be certain he was not followed – the Spanish police had owed the county force a favour.

Christmas Day on the island, once poorly celebrated except by the church, had, through the influence of television, expatriates and tourists, largely become the counterpart of that in many countries. In most hotels and many restaurants, turkey – sometimes with stuffing – roast potatoes, Brussels sprouts, Christmas pudding with rum butter, and wine, cava and brandy were served. Flowers took the place of paper chains, and the tops of small pine trees, Christmas trees.

Diana returned downstairs, went into the smoking room. 'She's asleep at last.'

'You look as if you wouldn't mind joining her,' Drury said.

'Recently, life's been so mentally fraught, I do feel exhausted.' She reached across to put her hand on his. 'Coming over has given us the perfect present.'

He smiled. 'Then I need not have bought the brooch.'

'Audrey has always said that your sense of humour stinks.'

*   *   *

The sun returned, the days became warm, the wind vanished, and the beaches were once more popular, although swimming was only for members of the polar club. Wendy was invited by her new friend to watch *The Three Kings*, and afterwards to a party. Having seen the caparisoned riders and the distribution of presents, her opinion that the family should move was confirmed.

THIRTEEN

Merriman was on night duty. Life had been pleasantly quiet and he was halfway through his stint and had started to look forward to returning home when the phone rang. *Typical*, he thought as he picked up the receiver.

'There's a missing girl report from Reetsham-by-Sea. Rose Stone, aged fifteen.'

'What do we know?'

'The mother phoned in to say Rose went with a friend to a party in town, here. The mother never sleeps until Rose returns home, and when it was three and the kid had not returned, she looked in the bedroom to confirm her daughter was not there. Sufficiently worried, she phoned the home of Susan, Rose's friend. Susan had left the party early because she had suddenly not felt very well. She had no idea where Rose was.'

'What's the parents' address?' Merriman asked.

'Fifteen, Rengton Street.'

Merriman replaced the receiver. Should he report to the DI before he checked that this was a genuine disappearance? It was a moot point. Waken Carren and it turn out to be a false alarm, and he could expect trouble; not report immediately and it proved to be a genuine disappearance, and he would be in the very deep end.

He checked the number in the directory, phoned Mrs Stone. Rose was still missing and something terrible must have happened to her . . . He did what was possible to calm her. He rang the detective inspector; Carren's anger at being woken was brief.

The age when Reetsham-by-Sea had been a popular seaside resort had passed many years before. Now, houses were often in need of repairs and painting, gardens were neglected, shops stocked few luxuries, and the ultimate indication of healthy trade, a supermarket, was absent.

In the street lighting, 15 Rengton Street, in the middle of
a terraced row, two up and two down, looked slightly less
shabby than it would have done in daylight. Mrs Stone, dressed
in a worn dressing-gown over pyjamas, was frantic with worry;
her husband, less so. He thought their daughter was . . . He
didn't need to spell it out. His wife was furious at the suggestion. Rose was a good daughter who always behaved herself
and knew how worried everyone would be if she didn't return
home at a reasonable time. That she hadn't, meant something
awful had happened to her . . .

Merriman left the house, settled in the CID car, phoned
Carren again to report Rose was still not at home, but that
the evidence failed to suggest whether or not she was missing
voluntarily.

Contact all hospitals, was Carren's first order.

On his return from Mallorca, Drury had moved back to
Parkside Farm, despite Audrey's insistence that he should
remain with them until Diana and Wendy arrived. He had
explained he was returning to chambers, so needed access
to his text and reference books, and to his law reports, when
he brought work home. This had provoked the remark that
he obviously needed to return to the hospital for another
brain scan.

The phone rang. He reached across to pick up the cordless
receiver, gave their phone number.

'Are you interested in—' the woman began.

'I'm sorry, I never respond to cold calls.'

'I never make 'em. Have you heard that a fifteen-year-old
girl has disappeared?'

'No.'

'Then I'm telling you.'

'Who are you?'

'Nostradamus. Predicting that if you give your evidence
in court, the next time you see her will be in a video showing
what happened before she had her throat cut with a butcher's
knife.'

The identification panel of the telephone showed the trans-
mission number had been blocked at source.

*   *   *

When Merriman had phoned, and her husband's reactions to the call had expressed fear and anger, Elaine Carren had panicked, certain their son was in serious trouble. Once forcibly assured that was not the case, mental relief had allowed her quickly to return to sleep. When she had woken, he had been snoring gently, and with a wifely regard for his well-being, but lack of respect for the demands of duty, she had not called him, and so he had not woken until long after it was time to go to work, a fault for which any junior would be severely castigated by him.

His annoyance was not improved when, on arrival at divisional HQ, he learned there had been no news as to Rose's whereabouts, and that Drury wanted to speak to him yet again and had been told to come to the station in a quarter of an hour's time.

'It didn't occur to you to allow me a little time to catch up with things?' he demanded.

Frenley looked at his watch.

'I had a very disturbed night.'

'Bad luck, sir.'

'Have Rose's friends been questioned to find out if they can say whether the girl was going strong with one of the boys at the party?'

'Enquiries are in progress, sir.'

'Can the Stones help?'

'The mother's half hysterical, and the father—'

The internal phone rang.

'Mr Drury is here to speak to you, sir.'

'Tell him to wait.' Carren replaced the receiver and continued to question Frenley about the steps which had been, and were about to be, taken to find the missing girl.

He went down to the front room and spoke to Drury. 'Sorry about the delay, but I had something which had to be finished p.d.q.'

'Has a fifteen-year-old girl disappeared locally?' Drury asked.

Carren concealed his surprise. 'Why do you ask?'

'A woman rang me before I came here. If I give my evidence in court, they will send me a video of a girl they have abducted which will show what happened to her before they murdered her.'

Carren stared at the wall. The answer to what would happen when it had become obvious Drury's wife and daughter had escaped the threat to blackmail him into silence was now apparent. 'What can you tell me about the voice of the woman who phoned you?'

'Very little. Initially I thought she was cold calling to try and sell me something, and that annoyed me. Then she made the threat and I was too confused and frightened by the idea she could be speaking the truth to note her voice.'

'You may have learned more than you realize. Was it an educated voice?'

'No.'

'Did it have an accent?'

'A kind of one, but I can't identify it.'

'Would you describe it as high or low pitched, or normal?'

'Normal.'

'Did she lisp? Pronounce words in an unusual way? Mix up Vs and Ws?'

'No.'

'You'll find this an unwelcome question, but might you have met her? Did she say anything that suggested she was in anyway familiar with your lifestyle?'

'No.'

There was a knock on the door and Merriman entered, crossed to the desk. 'Just received, sir.' He handed over a sheet of paper, then left.

'Is she still missing?' Drury asked.

Carren, who had been reading, looked up. 'I'm afraid so. She did not return home after a party.'

'Could she be with a friend?'

'Enquiries have shown that is not the case. Mr Drury, for now we have to accept the possibility that someone has kidnapped the girl in order to try to persuade you to lie in court.'

Drury's expression revealed his panicky horror. 'If I don't lie, they will treat her vilely before they murder her.'

'This could be a bluff.'

'How, when she is missing?'

'Regretfully, it frequently happens a girl goes missing.

Mostly, it's a voluntary disappearance – a family row, an unannounced sleepover. This may be such a one, yet those behind Fitch know that, until she turns up, they can use her disappearance to force you to do as they demand.'

'She'd have been in touch by now if she was free.'

'A sense of embarrassment might detain her. Remember something, Mr Drury; if she is captive, she is only of use to her captors whilst they can prove she is alive. Time is on our side until you have to go into the witness-box.'

'And if she isn't found by then?'

'I prefer to think she will be.'

'*You* aren't being asked to give evidence!'

'And, frankly, I hope to God I never am placed in such a position.'

There was a silence.

Carren spoke again. 'You will want your family to be with you, and that the girl has been kidnapped in order to force you to comply with their demands may make you believe they no longer consider harming your wife and daughter. Unfortunately, this isn't necessarily so. Rose Stone may escape, or she may die from an accident, or even from shock; or, however unlikely, a relationship may develop between captors and captive that inhibits any violence against her and even brings about her release. In which case, your family would again be at grave risk. So you must ask them not to return home.'

In Broadway Manor, Audrey was shocked by her brother's irresolution.

'If I lie, it might save her life,' Steven muttered. 'But I'll be on oath.'

Few people, she thought, still regarded an oath with irrefutable significance.

'I'll be betraying justice.'

'To have justice, one needs protection from the unjust.'

He ignored her. 'I've always done my damnedest to honour the law; it's like . . .' He could not find the word he needed.

'For you, a religion.'

'That's ridiculous.'

Was it? Her brother believed the law demanded total, uncritical loyalty from those who served it.

'How can I go into the witness-box and say I'm no longer certain the man I saw in the car park was Fitch; that I made a mistake with the photograph and at the identity parade? But if I don't, they'll carry out their threat: she'll be brutalized and murdered. Yet if I do, the girl may still be murdered to prevent her testifying against them. What the hell can I do?'

When the call was finally put through, a woman spoke Spanish at the speed of light. After she stopped, Drury said he wanted to speak to his wife. The woman did not respond. He could hear voices, otherwise he would have thought the line had been cut.

'Can I help you?' a man finally asked in English.

He repeated his request.

Another wait. Time stretched into infinity when one was about to do something one did not want to do.

'Steve?'

'I'm ringing—'

'We've had a slice of luck. We've managed to get two seats on a plane tomorrow. So unless you're appearing before the Lord Chief Justice, will you be at Gatwick at a quarter to twelve? And by way of celebration, let's have lunch at that restaurant halfway home where we had that delicious chocolate pudding last year.'

'I'm—'

She again interrupted him. 'Wendy says she wants two helpings.'

'I'm afraid it's off.'

'How on earth can you know they're not serving it tomorrow?'

'Your return has to be off.'

'What do you mean?'

'The police very strongly advise that you do not come back yet.'

'What the hell! Why?'

'In order to make me twist my evidence, and because

you are, thank God, beyond their reach, they've kidnapped a fifteen-year-old girl and told me she'll suffer hell if I don't change my evidence. If the police rescue her before the trial, you two could be come their target instead. I know how disappointing it must be when everything is arranged . . .'

'Are you going to change your evidence?'

'I . . . I don't know.'

There was a long pause.

'Her life must be saved,' she said.

'I know, but . . . it'll make me a criminal.'

'Only in your own mind. Surely you can say you were badly injured in the car park and you've realised that you had to be mentally confused so you are no longer able to swear to the identification?'

'I picked out the mugshot and named him at the identity parade.'

'Then you thought he looked similar to the man you saw that night, but now you realize you cannot swear it was he.'

'I have already given sworn evidence in the magistrates' court.'

'Which is more important? This girl's life or your religion?'

Carren phoned DCS Moss at county HQ. 'Drury received another threatening phone call last night, sir. A woman asked him if he knew a fifteen-year-old girl was missing. Told him that they had her and, if he gives the same evidence, she'll go through hell before they murder her.'

Moss swore.

'We're at full stretch, but there's precious little to go on. The only possible direct evidence we've learned is that a couple saw a girl walking ahead of them. A car stopped and the woman driver spoke to the girl, who then got into the car. Her mother swears her daughter would never accept a lift from a stranger, but it was a wet and windy night and likely Rose, if it was her, thought it must be safe because the driver was a woman. The odds are that Daisy Allen was the driver and it was she who phoned Drury to deliver the threat.'

'I'll come down.'

'Sir . . .'

'What?'

'I suggest it would be better if initially it is not you who questions Daisy.'

'Why?'

'As you may know, DC Park strikes a chord with her, and when they're fooling around—'

'In what way?' Moss demanded sharply.

'Verbally. Claiming invitations when they're not intended, that sort of thing. She might give something away to him. But if you or I open the questioning, she'll be on hard guard from the first word.'

'Has Drury listened to her speaking to see if he identifies her voice?'

'I thought it would be an idea for Park to talk to her with Mr Drury alongside.'

'Let me know the result immediately.'

Ingham was off duty; unwanted time since it meant he was at home. He used the remote to switch the television to the news. The weather forecast offered snow showers to the west of the country.

'Feels cold enough to have 'em here,' he said.

Jane remained silent.

He looked across at her in the other easy chair. She was cross-stitching a complex pattern which demanded her close attention. He guessed it gave her reason to be fully occupied when he was around. She had returned home from her friend Moira's, but she had hardly said a word to him since; he was evidently very much *not* forgiven.

It had been her inner sparkle that had immediately attracted him. There was no sparkle now. She was tired, dispirited, bitter. For the hundredth time, he tried and failed to understand how he could have thought what he did. That she had frequently complained, with increasing bitterness, about the interruptions to their social life his work caused, and that she had accused him of wrecking their anniversary, was no excuse . . .

The television broke into his harsh thoughts.

'The police are asking anyone who may have seen Rose

Stone, or who has any information that may concern her, to get in touch with them immediately.'

'Poor kid,' he muttered.

Jane briefly looked up, resumed stitching.

FOURTEEN

'Never give up, do you?' Daisy Allen said bitterly as she stood in the doorway of her house.

'Not when the prize is worth the effort,' Park replied.

'Who's he?' She pointed at Drury.

'With me for a bit.'

'Then he's bleeding unlucky.'

'Are you asking us in?'

'No.'

'It's cold out here. Cold enough to have 'em drop off.'

'Wouldn't have thought you'd any to drop.'

'I'll show you how wrong you are.'

'You'll clear off.'

'You're going to have to talk to us.'

'Been doing nothing else.'

'Leave us out here and it'll be the big cheese who next wants a chat.'

'I'm shivering.'

'Not as much as we are. He'll take you apart because he reckons you can help him increase his conviction rate.'

'I ain't done nothing, and no one can prove different.'

'As I said to him, you're a sparky lady, but in with the wrong mob.'

'Like now.'

'And he said—' He stopped.

'What?'

'Ask us in before my tongue freezes and I'll tell you.'

'Bugger off.'

'Lovely lady, have I got to get all formal and ask you to be kind enough to come along to have a chat at the – I won't use the words you favour – station?'

She left the door open, retreated into the front room.

'No idea what peaceful co-operation means.' Park spoke quietly. 'Well, Mr Drury, does she sound like the woman who phoned you?'

'The rhythms and intonations of her speech are similar, but I couldn't swear it was she.'

'A pity. But that's the way things go. Thanks for your help.'

Drury walked back to his car, which was parked behind the CID Escort.

Park went into the house. Daisy was standing by the window, the panes of which were patterned with dust. 'Where's the other one going?' she demanded.

'He's warm-hearted and sussed that you wanted to be on your own with me.'

'He looked at me like I couldn't make a couple of quid in a back street.'

'You mistake scorn for passion. He didn't dare stay here or his feelings would have overcome him.' He settled on the settee, patted the empty half. 'Come and sit down and talk to uncle.'

'My uncle is a dirty old man with bad breath who can't keep his hands to himself, but I'd rather sit with him than with you.'

'You're being very unkind. I'm here to help you, Daisy.'

'You don't help anyone but yourself.'

'You know you're in trouble.'

'Dan was with me, up in the smoke, and you can't prove different.'

'I'm not here because of that.'

Her concerned surprise was immediate, but quickly suppressed.

'Been travelling recently, Daisy?'

'No.'

'Visiting your dear old grandmother?'

'They was both lucky. Died before you was around.'

'What say we talk about you driving around last night to find out what was on offer?'

She ignored the question.

'I did some phoning before I came here. The DVLA says you run a Seat Panda and have a recently renewed driving licence.'

'What are you getting at?'

'Your car was seen on the outskirts of town on Thursday night.'

FlashScan System

City of San Diego Public Library
Central Library
** ********************************

1/2/2013 3:52:05 PM
Title: Criminal innocence
Item ID: 31336087471372
Date Due: 1/23/2013,23:59

1 item

Renew at www.sandiegolibrary.org
OR Call 619 236-5800 or 858 484-4440
and press 1 then 3 to RENEW.
Your library card is needed
to renew borrowed items.

'So that's where the bastard was after he'd nicked it.'

'You're suggesting it was stolen?'

'Yes.'

'When?'

'A time ago.'

'You reported the theft?'

'When you lot aren't interested unless it's from one of your own?'

'Funny you're still using it.'

'It turned up. Must have been a joyrider having fun with someone else's petrol.'

'You have a mobile phone.'

'What if I have?'

'It was used on Thursday night, very close to where the young girl was snatched.'

'What young girl?'

'You don't listen to the news? Did Dan tell you to grab the first kid fool enough to walk home on her own at night?'

'Dan?'

'Fitch.'

'How's he going to tell me anything when he's banged up?'

'Never been explained to you how to slip messages into and out of the nick?'

'Don't listen to that sort of talk.'

'You want me to believe you didn't have anything to do with the snatch, even though you were in the right area at the right time? Come on, Daisy. You were in your car, likely with someone hiding in the back, ready to keep the kid quiet as soon as she was inside. You're right in the frame.'

'And you're as full of shit as ever. The telly said the coppers weren't making any progress in finding her.'

'I thought you didn't know who I was talking about?'

She looked briefly at him with open hostility.

'And you believe what they say on the telly? You'll be trusting the papers next. We weren't going to give anything away this early on and say there were two witnesses.'

She stood, crossed to the littered mantelpiece, and picked up a pack of cigarettes. 'Hoping to bum one?' she sneered.

'Gave up smoking years ago when I decided to lead a clean life.'

She tapped a cigarette out of the pack, lit it, and returned to her chair.

'They saw Rose Stone get into a Seat Panda. *Your* car's a Seat Panda.'

'So are thousands of others. And, like I said, mine was nicked.'

'They saw your face when you spoke to the girl through the opened window and asked her if she'd like a lift out of the rain.'

'When some of the street lighting wasn't working?'

'How do you know that?'

'Said it on the telly.'

'Never mentioned. You're all scrambled. Daisy, why do I have to keep telling you I want to help you? The evidence can see you inside for a lifer. When a young girl has been kidnapped and threatened with rape and worse, the jury knows its verdict before the evidence is heard; the judge wonders if he can hand out something more than a life sentence without remission. But there is one way of making the best of things. Shouldn't be telling you this, of course, but I don't want to have to think of you in jail. Tell the truth and express repentance. Judges like to think that their pomp and circumstance have produced a repentant confessor. And when you're asked if you've anything to say before sentence is pronounced, weep a tear, explain you had to do as ordered or you'd have been hanged, drawn and quartered. That'll get the judge thinking maybe a little community service would make the punishment fit the crime.'

'You think I'm so soft, I'll believe that crap?'

'I am merely trying to . . .'

'Make me dig me own grave.'

'I'm sorry you think that.'

She stubbed out her cigarette.

'The evidence against you is too tight to try to fight.'

'There ain't any, since it wasn't me in the car.'

'You were out at night, looking for a young kid to snatch.'

She stood, went over to the fireplace, and lit another cigarette.

'And when you'd found one, you used your mobile to let Fitch's mate know.'

'You're into fairy stories.'

'Only when they don't contain fairies. Where's your mobile?'

'Nicked. A kid showed me a knife, and there wasn't any of you lot around because you're always too busy running after innocents.'

'You must be tired of having stuff pinched.'

She flicked ash on to the floor.

'They gave me the number of your mobile.' He produced his. 'What was your number?'

'Can't remember.'

He dialled. A few bars of tinny music, which he didn't recognize, sounded from the clutter on the mantelpiece.

'Seems like it wasn't stolen and you've been telling a porky.'

'I saw the kid again what snatched it. Told him I'd run him in if he didn't hand it back.'

Park reported to the detective inspector and Sergeant Frenley.

'Mr Drury had a good chance of listening to her, sir.'

'And?' Carren asked.

'It could have been her because of the nature of her speaking, but he can't swear it was.'

'As much use as a dead goldfish.'

'Before I went with Mr Drury, I had a chat with the mobile people, reckoning Daisy would use a mobile when she was on the hunt. They told me her phone had been used about the time we think Rose was snatched and around where she would have been when walking home. I told Daisy two witnesses had watched the kid get into her car and had seen her face. She didn't buy it.'

'You expected her to?'

'Might have done after I'd explained how she could do herself good by confessing. Denied she'd been out in her car Thursday evening; said it had been taken by a joyrider who'd returned it when he'd had his fun. I said her mobile had been used when the kid was snatched; *she* said it had been nicked by a kid with a knife. So I used mine to dial the number I'd been given by the operating company. Her mobile rang loud and clear. So her story changed, and now she claimed she'd seen the kid again and made him return it.'

'Can we prove her car was not used for joyriding; that her mobile was not stolen; and that she hadn't faced the yob who'd mugged her of her phone and retrieved it?'

'No. But it's too unlikely a story to carry weight.'

'In five minutes, a really sharp counsel would prove nothing could be more likely.' Carren adjusted his toupee, as he often did when worried, and was briefly annoyed to note Park had been watching. 'I've been remembering a case from my beginning at the job. A woman was grabbed by the man she refused to marry. He disappeared along with her. Enquiries showed she had a passion for Cadbury's Dairy Milk chocolate and some smart DC decided to check out if any shops in the likely area of her imprisonment were selling an unusual number of bars of that chocolate. Sounds like a drowning man's grab for a straw, but it paid off. Her captor was buying a dozen bars at a time. And that brought him into view. I wonder . . .' He became silent.

Getting desperate, Park decided.

Might as well consult a crystal ball, Frenley thought.

'At this stage,' Carren said, 'they'll be doing what they can to keep her peaceful and quiet. So question the parents, find out her particular likes. What's her favourite food? Does she read a lot of books, and if so, who's her favourite author? That sort of thing. You understand?'

'Yes, but . . . I just wonder if . . .'

'What?'

'It does seem rather a . . . strange way to go about trying to find her.'

'I don't remember asking for your judgment.'

As he lay in bed, Drury heard the post-office van turn into the drive, the crunch of feet on the gravel, the snap of the interior lid of the post box closing. He looked at his watch. It was early, but thinking, hoping, worrying, did not make for a pleasant lie-in. He climbed out of bed, walked into the small, en-suite bathroom, the space of which was severely limited by the sloping peg-tile roof. He bathed, dressed, and went downstairs, picking up the mail on his way to the kitchen, and then filled and switched on the coffee machine, hesitated whether to have bacon and egg. He 'heard' Audrey's warning that fried food would send his cholesterol level sky-high, and in a spirit of sensible but unwelcome self-denial, decided on toast and marmalade.

In the dining room, the cast-iron fireback and wrought-iron firedogs in the inglenook fireplace were thick with dust. They had not been touched since Diana had left. Daily-Two would never dust them because she believed that to do so would make the devil welcome. As he ate, he checked the mail. All but two letters were dustbin material. One of the remaining two was an invitation to the wedding of the daughter of acquaintances rather than friends. The remaining envelope was slightly bulky. Inside was a tuft of blonde hair, dark at the roots. Surprise was succeeded by bitter fear.

Carren held the envelope by his fingertips; the possibility of a pertinent print was remote, but any that were raised by Forensics would have to be checked.

Frenley, standing in front of the desk, said, 'They've spelt the name of the village wrong. Could be useful if the writer makes the same mistake when questioned.'

Carren dropped the envelope and tuft of hair into an exhibit bag. 'Unfortunately, we don't yet have confirmation this hair came from Rose Stone, do we?'

'No, sir.'

'Can't be much doubt, but check. The classic first move to persuade prompt payment – or, in this case, altered testimony.' He drummed on the desk with his fingers. 'I'd judge Drury to be a man who tries to tell the truth, whatever the circumstances. But she's a fifteen-year-old girl and the threat is to rape, torture, kill. How is he going to respond?'

'He'll have to lack imagination or compassion to be able to ignore the threat.'

'In other words, he'll find he can't identify Fitch after all?'

'In the circumstances, would you?'

Carren stopped drumming. 'What is the probability of the verdict if he finds he can no longer identify Fitch?'

'We've very little evidence that isn't circumstantial. On top of that, we can't judge if the court will allow any evidence concerning the "not guilty" trial of Fitch in Cumbria. Even if it does, it's only surmise that Fitch posed as a member of the CID to gain entry into Donaldson's place. Drury's evidence is the cornerstone. Take that away and the case may well collapse.'

'Do we tackle Daisy Allen again?'

'Park says he tried everything he could think of to get her to come aboard, and she just laughed at him.'

'What's motivating her? Affection for, or fear of, Fitch?'

'Maybe the first, but certainly the last.'

'So she goes into court providing an alibi we can't shake; nor may we impugn her character unless the defence say she's as white as snow. We know she was almost certainly in the car that kidnapped the girl in order to pressure Drury, but cannot prove it . . . The rules of evidence were drawn up by friends of the guilty.' He stood, walked around his desk and across to the window, and stared out at the overcast grey sky, the light drizzle, and the hurrying men and women who, he thought, would have little concern for those who were not their own family and friends. Perhaps he, Frenley, Park, Ingham, and Merriman should not allow themselves to be emotionally disturbed by the case. None of them knew Rose Stone. Were she to die in an accident, her death would go unremarked by them. Yet it had been written that no man was an island. 'If Fitch escapes a guilty verdict, do you think they will release Rose?'

'I can't see that. They may have kept her blindfolded, cut off her hearing, but she must have seen the driver of the car full face. They'll keep her while she's of use, then they'll get rid of her.'

'Which means that if Drury does sacrifice his self-respect and career by lying in the witness box, it'll prove to have been useless. Do you think he realizes that?'

'He's been in the business long enough to know how villains work.'

'She's dead unless we find her before Drury gives evidence at the trial?'

'I can't see it any other way, sir.'

'Neither can I,' Carren said harshly.

FIFTEEN

Drury picked out the two slices of toast from the toaster and put them into the rack, and then hurried through to the hall, and lifted the receiver.

'It's Audrey. I just wanted to . . . Dammit, I know what I want to say, but not how to put it. Everyone will understand that whatever your evidence, you gave it because you had to.'

'Dishonour rooted in honour?'

'You won't accept that's true?'

'I suppose I have to.' Yet he could be certain that whatever action he took, it would not save Rose Stone. Only finding her would do that. If that did not happen, at the end of the trial, whatever the verdict, she was doomed . . . unless he could find a way of making the impossible, possible.

'If only you could . . .'

'Be more down to earth? Accept that the truth is often twisted whenever doing so offers an advantage? That we live in a time when those in power have taught us the end always justifies the means?'

'I think I should not have rung. Come and have dinner with us tonight?'

'It's very kind, but—'

'Roast pheasant with mother's secret sauce; lemon-meringue pie.'

'Condemned men always had their chosen meal *before* they were hanged, not after.'

'I expect you here by . . . When does the court pack up?'

'Difficult to be certain.'

'You're being equally difficult yourself. By eight o'clock at the latest.'

He said goodbye, replaced the receiver, wished he had been able to show a more grateful response to her kindness.

Rose Stone's mother possessed the mental backbone her husband lacked. Throughout their married life, it had been

she who had made the difficult decisions. She answered
Ingham's questions while her husband seemed unable to do
anything but seek sympathy for the terrible situation in which
he was embroiled.

'You want to know if she had a particular liking for a
computer game. Why?' Mrs Stone asked.

'If she has always enjoyed them, Mrs Stone, this might
give us a lead.'

'How?'

Stone said, 'She ain't got a player. Wanted us to buy her
one. Ain't got the money for that kind of stupidity.'

'That answers one question, then.' Ingham spoke to Mrs
Stone. 'Does she read a lot?'

'What's it matter?' Stone muttered. 'You ain't going to
find her.'

'There's no reason to think that.'

'We ain't going to see her again, not ever.'

'Give over, Dad,' Mrs Stone said sharply. She faced Ingham.
'Reads as many books as she can get out of the library.'

'What kind – adventure? Romance? Witches and wizards?'

'Much anything that has a beginning and an end. Why
you asking?'

'Her captors could be borrowing books from the public
library to keep her as quiet as possible.' He tried to sound
as if he believed that. Privately, he thought this way of gaining
a lead was nonsense. Yet he'd have to speak to the library
staff and ask if anyone had been borrowing books on Rose's
behalf because she was ill . . . 'Does she have to have any
medicine regularly?'

'Not really.'

'How'd you mean?'

'Had a weak stomach and often felt sick since she was
young. Then the doctor said she ought to drink cranberry
juice regular and it helped her so now she has it every
day.'

He half-listened to a long and detailed list of Rose's
medical complaints and repeated references to cranberry
juice.

'Costs a fortune,' Stone muttered.

'You resent her being fit?' Mrs Stone demanded angrily.

She turned to Park. 'She won't have none now, and she'll be frantic, like when she lost Jumbo.'

'Jumbo?'

'Had a toy elephant that she carried everywhere when she was real young. It went missing once and she was in a terrible state about it. Not having the juice will get her so upset . . . You see, to her it's become a kind of . . . of something that means she won't be ill.'

Ingham asked a few more questions of little consequence, and then left the house and its sad, bitter atmosphere. He settled in the CID car, used the radio to call divisional HQ, spoke to Frenley. 'I've talked to the Stones, sarge, and all I've learned is the girl regularly drinks some kind of juice for her health.'

'Orange? Lemon? Peach?'

'Begins with a C . . . cranberry. The mother told me, not the father. He's a mournful prat. Seems Rose had gut trouble from very young and the juice stops that. The mother says Rose will be in a hell of a state without it, reckoning she's about to collapse.'

'So maybe they're getting it for her. Find out where it's sold locally and whether anyone's been buying it in unusual quantity.'

'Seems a waste of time that could better be sent searching for her.'

Ingham spoke to the assistant manager of Asda supermarket, explained the reason for the questions.

'You want to know if we sell cranberry juice? Yes. Can we trace any unusual sale of it to a customer by searching till records, speaking to the staff and so on? A mammoth task with every chance of getting nowhere, even if it's possible. However, obviously, I'll do what I can.'

'Thanks.'

'No thanks needed if it'll help the girl.'

Ingham spoke to the manager of Sainsbury's supermarket. His reception was similar to the previous one. The library assistant, meanwhile, was surprised that Ingham could believe a single book, DVD or tape would be loaned without an appropriate library ticket; there could be no exception, even on the grounds of sickness. Rules were made in order that they should be obeyed.

The Crown Court in Kurston was housed in a large building, fronted by six ionic columns. In Victorian times, it had been thought correct to provide the law with the trappings of power and majesty.

Drury folded *The Times*; his brain refused to make lasting sense of what he was reading. He stared at the patterned marble floor as he finally accepted what he would have to do; yet, unavailingly, he sought a way of avoiding doing it.

Mr Justice Horricks was in a black gown since it was not a red-letter day. He was noted for his sharp intelligence, his precise summings-up, and his politeness to witnesses. He listened to Querry's opening speech – ten words being made to do the job of one – and was grateful, without hinting by word or expression that this was so, when its conclusion was reached. The first witness was called.

'Constable, will you please tell the court what happened shortly after midnight on Monday, the eight of November?'

'I learned that an alarm had sounded at Donaldson, the jewellers, on High Street. I was to the south of there and made my way to the building. As I approached, a car drove very quickly out of the small employees' car park behind the nearby supermarket. I was unable to distinguish the registration number. I reported events as I made my way to the square.'

'Square?'

'Car park, sir.'

Querry adjusted the set of his gown; as a QC, it was silk, in contrast to his junior's gown, which was stuff. 'What did you find in the car park?'

'There was a man lying on the ground.'

'Initially, what did you imagine was the cause of his being there?'

'There is a nearby public house, and I thought he was drunk. As I stood there, he began to moan, and I switched on my torch and determined he had been injured. I called an ambulance. As I waited for that to arrive, I asked where he lived, if he was married, who should be contacted. He had difficulty in speaking but, before the ambulance arrived, I was able to understand his wife was away and his sister lived in town. After some attempts, he succeeded in telling me her address.'

Querry turned and spoke briefly to his junior. He faced the witness box again. 'Thank you, constable.' He sat.

One row behind, Brooke, acting for the defence, stood. A junior counsel, he had an uninspiring appearance and at times a seemingly hesitant manner – facts that caused some witnesses to treat him with a measure of contempt. A mistake, they soon learned.

'Constable, you thought he was drunk. Why was that?'

'He would not have been the first drunk I found in the area.'

'You could not mark any difference in the circumstances?'

'He was just lying there.'

'So you have said. What I am asking is, were you not able to note his obvious signs of distress?'

'Not before he began to moan and I switched on my torch.'

'Why not?'

'It wouldn't have been of any use.'

'I don't follow you, constable.'

'The light was too poor to make out any details.'

'The light was too poor to make out any details,' Brooke repeated slowly and with emphasis.

The court adjourned.

Carren left his room and walked along to Frenley's. 'Anything from Reetsham-by-Sea?'

Frenley, who had been working on his computer, sat back in his chair. 'I rang half an hour ago, sir. No joy so far. The two witnesses who saw the girl get into the car haven't been able to dredge up anything more, and it's reckoned there's no chance of obtaining any fresh evidence from them; supermarkets are studying records and asking staff about a large purchase of cranberry juice, but reckon this will take a long time and will probably fail. It does look like it's a very long shot. The villains may have had the

sense to buy one carton at a time from a different store, if
they've bought it at all.'

'I doubt that. They won't want to be seen all over the place.
I want Park to talk to that woman again.'

'Sir.'

'All right, you don't have to point out she's been questioned several times and not given anything away.'

'Could it be any good offering—' He stopped suddenly.
'Forget it, sir.'

'Were you about to suggest the case is dropped against
Fitch if she gives us evidence that'll lead us to Rose?'

'Something like that,' Ingham confessed.

'In a murder case?'

'I . . . It's just . . .'

'I know what you're trying to say. It's likely even
Superintendent Moss has thought along similar lines before
rejecting the idea as completely impractical, not to say thoroughly illegal. Reaching the top of the greasy pole doesn't
isolate one from emotions.'

'No, sir.' Frenley was silent, then said with angry passion,
'There's no room! If Drury goes into the box and tells the
truth, Fitch gets banged up and Rose is murdered; but if
Drury lies and Fitch goes free, Rose is still murdered.'

'We have to hope something turns up in time.'

'What time? The trial's under way. Prosecuting counsel has
given his bellyful of an opening speech, and the witnesses are
being called. We've followed every possible and impossible
lead to no effect. I'd like to put thumbscrews on Daisy!'

'And I'd like to tighten them.'

'For Christ's sake, not again,' Daisy said bitterly as she stood
in the open doorway of her house.

'Don't blame me for hoping,' Park answered.

'Hope yourself stupid and it still won't do any good.'

'I need to talk.'

'I don't need to listen.'

'Ask me in and I'll invite you to the police ball next month.'

'Don't go dancing with scavengers.'

He stepped into the house, causing her to move aside.

'I'll have you for illegal entry.'

'I'd prefer it normal.' He went into the front room.

She followed him.

'Let's save time. Tell me the truth about that Monday night and grow a halo.'

'I was with Dan at the theatre and restaurant, stayed the night with him at the hotel. And you've no bleeding right to have him inside.'

'Not responsible. I just learn the truth and pass it on. Needs a judge to hand out a hundred and fifty years of living at the state's expense . . . Drury will be in the witness box very soon.'

'He'll lie.'

'And you'll become an accomplice to murder.'

'Still trying that one?'

'Have you thought about how Rose must be suffering?'

'Better things to do.'

'She was unlucky enough to be in the wrong place at the wrong time when you were looking for a girl you could snatch in an effort to save a brutal murderer.'

'You're boring me.'

'She's only fifteen.'

She shrugged her shoulders.

'Being held in frightening conditions.'

'At fifteen, my dad had cleared off, my mum was dying, and I was having to nick grub if I wanted to eat. You won't make me weep because of what's happening to some kid I ain't never clapped eyes on.'

'If she's held, sexually molested and then murdered, we'll be after you so fast you won't see us coming.'

'When you can't prove nothing?'

'Seems you don't understand. You escape this one and you'll be stitched up for something else.'

She said scornfully, 'You come here with a sob story and then threaten me? You ain't out of shorts yet.'

Twenty minutes later, Park reported to Frenley. 'I did the best I could, sarge, but it was a total waste of time.'

'Had to be likely. There's nothing more we can do. Even when we know what's going to happen to her.'

*   *   *

For once, Drury managed to park reasonably close to Broadway Manor. Audrey opened the front door of the flat. 'Well?'

'I've not been called,' he answered as he stepped inside.

'Do you know when you will be?'

'Probably tomorrow morning.'

'Has anything changed?'

'No.'

She touched his arm, a rare physical example of the close ties between them. 'Have you—' She stopped.

'Decided what to do, when whatever I do will result in her death?'

SIXTEEN

Ingham returned to the CID room.

'Any joy?' Merriman asked quickly.

'Not even a hint of it. The supermarkets are doing all they can, but it's negative reports from all of them so far.'

'They did say it would take time.'

'Which we haven't got.'

Merriman yawned. 'I haven't rung Phillipa to say I'd be tied up. She'll give me hell for forgetting.'

'It's not all that late.'

'I'm hanging on for a while in case something breaks.'

The phone on Ingham's desk rang and he knew sudden hope as he lifted the receiver. 'CID. DC Ingham speaking.'

'It's Simkins here. Don't suppose you remember me?'

'You're the manager at Tesco near the Wainwright monument. Have you managed to find an unusual sale of juice?'

'Afraid not. But there is something that might be of interest to you.'

'What is it?'

'I'd handed over to my relief who does night duty and was walking across to my car outside the store when I met a man I knew quite well, but hadn't seen recently because he lives a few miles out of town. He wanted to know if it was true we'd been asked to try to find an unusual sale of cranberry juice; when I told him it was, and that we weren't getting anywhere, he said his family always bought it from their local store to try and help it remain profitable despite the competition from us supermarkets. His wife drinks cranberry juice for her health, so sometime back he persuaded the shop to stock it. Very recently, she went there to buy a couple of cartons of juice and was told someone had come in and bought up all they had. The shop had ordered fresh stock, but it hadn't arrived yet . . . Probably doesn't mean a thing, but I thought I'd mention it.'

'Glad you did. Where is this shop?'

'Tilting Green.'

'Can you give the name of it?'

'Palmer Stores. As it's the only shop in the village, there's no mistaking it.'

Ingham thanked Simkins and promised to let him know if the information proved to be of any value.

'Something?' Merriman asked hopefully.

'Fingers crossed.' He made his way to Frenley's room, reported.

'Tilting Green,' Frenley said. 'Some reckon there was once tilting there, others say that's a load of rubbish. You'd better get yourself there and find out if there's anything to this.'

Ingham left the building and took the CID car. Normally careful, his excited hope caused him to drive recklessly.

Tilting Green, once a very small village, was becoming larger as houses were built along the ridge of higher ground. At the T-junction, he turned right, and almost immediately came in sight of the store. Blinds had been drawn over the single window and the half-glassed door. He walked round the corner and found a small open area in which was parked a van; to his left was a door marked 'Private'. He knocked.

The door was opened by a man of small height, whose head was crowned with curling brown hair. 'The shop is closed. What is it?' he asked resentfully.

'Constable Ingham, county CID. You are . . .?'

'Jenkins.'

'Sorry to trouble you, Mr Jenkins, but I had a phone call from Mr Simkins. He told me something that may be important.'

'The cranberry juice?'

'Yes.'

'Please come inside.'

Jenkins opened a door to the side of a staircase, switched on an overhead light and led the way into the shop.

'Thought it would be better in here, Constable. The family's upstairs, and I reckoned you'd prefer a bit of quiet.'

They stood by the counter.

'As I have it, recently someone came in and bought all the

cranberry juice you had in stock,' Ingham said. 'Is that the way it was?'

'Yes.'

'Was it a man or a woman?'

'Man.'

'Did you know him?'

'Never clapped eyes on him before.'

'How many cartons of juice did he take?'

'Eight or nine. Can't remember exactly.'

'Did he buy anything else?'

'Tins of this and that, all the bread I had, sealed cheese and meat, two packs of lager and a bottle of whisky. He wanted more whisky, but I hadn't any. Needed three cardboard boxes to carry it all. I asked him if he was off sailing around the world, but he never said anything.'

'Has he been back?'

'No.'

'Any idea where he's living?'

'He said what he wanted, I told what he owed, tried small talk but was ignored, and he paid. That was our conversation.'

'Was he in a car?'

'Yes.'

'Did you notice the make and colour? What about the registration number?'

'I've no idea. Just heard it drive off, that's all.'

Ingham rubbed an irritation on his neck. 'He'll likely come back for more grub.'

'When he took enough to keep well fed for weeks?'

'Maybe he isn't on his own . . . We're going to need your help, Mr Jenkins.'

'Roy said the cranberry juice was to do with the missing girl. Is that right?'

'It is.'

'Then count on me for all you want.'

'I'm about to!' Ingham smiled. 'I'd like you to come in to town and help us draw up a computer-graphic portrait of the man.'

'Name the time and I'll be there.'

Ingham left the shop, sat behind the wheel of the car, and used the radio to report his meeting with Jenkins.

'How do you see it?' Frenley asked.

'Looks like we're going to have to wait for this man to return to stock up with more provisions, booze and juice. There'll be more than one of 'em, – the kidnappers, I mean – so even if the grub lasts, the booze won't, and likely the girl's drinking juice by the gallon. If Jenkins gives us the wink and holds the man there long enough, we'll be able to follow him.'

'It's countryside, isn't it?'

'Yes.'

'Then it'll be near impossible to shadow without being eyeballed.'

'Won't they be so certain everything's going smoothly, the driver won't be keeping an eye open?'

'They're professionals. And how long can they be kept at the shop? Any obvious and unnecessary delay and their alarm bells will be ringing.'

'Get the county helicopter overhead to watch where they drive.'

'When we don't know when it'll be needed, so that it has to be on constant immediate standby at some unimaginable cost to us?'

'Sarge, we look like we've been given a chance. We have to grab it or the girl's dead.'

Carren spoke to Moss at County HQ, detailed the fresh information.

'How long have we got?' Moss asked.

'It's difficult to judge when Drury will be called.'

'We must have an estimate.'

'Querry is, by reputation, long-winded. Forensic blokes have to be called and so do our lads. A guesstimate is Friday.'

'That early?'

'There's little hard evidence for counsel to waste their time arguing about.'

'And we have to bank on the kidnappers needing to replenish their supplies in time.'

'It could be soon, sir. They may have bought a lot of stuff, but they'll be bored and likely eating and drinking heavily. Another thing; if Rose finds relief, hope, whatever you like to call it, from cranberry juice, she'll very soon need more.'

'Then how do you suggest we go about marking them?'

'With a tracker unit.'

'Planted on their car? How do we know when the car will be outside the shop?'

'We fix a lad in one of the houses that overlook Palmer Stores. Jenkins tells the villain he needs to get something from the storeroom and, while in there, gives our man the buzz. He walks across to the car and plants the unit.'

'You're assuming he won't be watched from the moment he approaches the car.'

'Not if he's kitted out like some dozy farmhand. How does it sound, sir?'

'Like challenging fate.'

SEVENTEEN

M r Justice Horricks entered the courtroom. Lawyers and public stood; he sat, they sat. He leaned forward in order to speak briefly to the clerk of the court, then sat upright. 'Mr Querry.'

'Yes, My Lord?'

'You are ready to proceed?'

'I am, My Lord.'

'Very well.'

'Mr Delaney,' Querry said.

Those inside could hear the name being called outside the courtroom. Delaney entered, walked to the witness box, took the oath.

'You are James Eric Delaney and you live in Ravenglass?'

'That is so.'

'What is your occupation?'

'I am the owner and editor of the *Drigg Gazette*.' He was an earnest man by nature – earnest by appearance, earnest in manner; someone who would search hard and long for something that was not in its usual place, even if he did not need it.

'That is a local paper with a restricted circulation?'

'It will be better to allow the witness to give the evidence,' the judge remarked.

'Yes, My Lord ... Mr Delaney, is the *Gazette* a daily or weekly newspaper?'

'Weekly.'

'Would you describe it as widely read?'

'That depends on the terms of reference. Many people who live in and around Ravenglass read it; in comparison with a national newspaper, however, it is not.'

'Will you describe the nature of your paper?'

' 'It tries to keep the past remembered. It explains local customs, both extant and extinct, and how they arose; it notes words peculiar to the area and what they mean; it gives traditional recipes; carries social information – weddings, silver and golden anniversaries – and news concerning people who have left the area and what they are presently doing; it provides reports of events that took place in the past week and notices of events to come.'

'Would you agree that your paper will be of considerable interest to someone who lives or has lived in the area, who knows it from visits, or who is familiar with many who live in it, but is of less interest to anyone who does not?'

'I think that is correct.'

'If I expressed an interest in receiving the *Gazette* here, in the south, would a newsagent order it for me?'

'That is very unlikely, since it would not be in his financial interest to do so.'

'And if I lived in Birmingham?'

'I am reasonably certain a newsagent would not accept the order.'

'And in Carlisle?'

'Are we,' the judge asked, 'to cover towns in Scotland and Wales as well as in England?'

'My Lord, I am establishing the fact that the *Drigg Gazette* is not a nationally available newspaper.'

'The jury will no doubt have appreciated that fact.'

Provided eleven of them were more intelligent than the woman in the back row, Querry thought. She obviously couldn't understand, and wasn't interested in, what was going on. 'Mr Delaney, to be specific, as His Lordship wishes, is it correct to say that if I am living here, I would normally never see a copy of the *Drigg Gazette*?'

'That is correct.'

'But if I know someone who lives near Drigg and its neighbouring villages – including, of course, Ravenglass and Devil's Hillside – she or he might well send me a copy out of interest?'

'I imagine that frequently happens.'

'Do you remember the contents of the issue dated the fifth of September this year?'

'I am afraid not.'

'Will you look at what the usher hands you?'

'I am to receive a copy of the document?' the judge asked. 'And the jury also?'

'Yes, My Lord.'

Querry was silent until judge and witness each had a copy of a page from the newspaper. 'Can you identify from what that came?'

'The *Drigg Gazette*?'

'Mr Querry,' the judge said, 'the first third of the page that I have has been blacked out. Are the jury's copies and the witnesses' in similar conditions?'

'Yes, My Lord.'

The judge examined the page under the light by his side; twice, he reversed the page.

Brooke stood. 'My Lord, I object to the introduction of this evidence.'

'On what grounds?'

'It has the potential of being inferentially detrimental to my client.'

'Is he mentioned by name?'

'No.'

'Is there anything printed that might reasonably be thought to refer to the accused?'

'The fact that part of the report is deleted suggests something was printed that might be considered detrimental to him.'

'Since we cannot know what has been expunged, it might equally be considered it was of a complimentary nature and so has been deleted in order not to present a biased opinion.'

'That seems unlikely, My Lord.'

'Then you have reason to believe the hidden words must be detrimental to your client?'

Brooke sat.

Querry ran a finger around the inside of his starched wing collar to try to stop it digging into his neck. 'Mr Delaney, can you identify who was the author of this article?'

'I wrote it.'

'Will you now tell the jury what is the subject of the article, making no reference to anything that is not in print in front of you.'

'It concerns an attempted robbery near Drigg, following a number of robberies in the area. A man dressed in a police constable's uniform entered a large house, after claiming he

had been ordered to make a security check on the alarm
systems in properties that could be considered possible
targets. The owner of the house, a local magistrate, recognized him to be a bogus PC. The man fled, but police were
called and later arrested him.'

'Was he tried in court?'

'Yes.'

'What was the verdict?'

'Not guilty.'

'The evidence for the prosecution was found to be insufficient or faulty?'

'Two friends provided an alibi.'

'Were the friends male or female?'

'Female.'

'Do you remember their names?'

'You will not answer that question, Mr Delaney,' the judge
said. He spoke to Querry. 'I made it quite clear where the
boundaries lay.'

'Yes, My Lord.'

Querry turned and spoke quietly to his junior. 'Crabby
bastard!' He turned back, leaned forward to speak briefly to
his instructing solicitor, then sat.

Brooke rose. 'The *Drigg Gazette* may not be readily available in many parts of the country, but that does not mean
someone in such areas is unable to read your paper. They
can subscribe to have it sent to their home?'

'We do not have a subscription service.'

Brooke silently swore, but his expression remained
unchanged. 'But as we have heard, someone who lives within
your readership area may, of course, send a copy of your paper
to a relative or friend who has reason to enjoy reading it?'

'Yes.'

'Thank you.' Brooke sat.

Querry did not re-examine.

For once, PC Erwin considered himself to be a lucky man.
Nearbrook Cottage – ragstone walls, thatched roof, leaded
windows and small garden – was the property of his dreams.
So very different from the dull, characterless house in which
he and Sally, his wife, lived. Miss Osborn, who owned the

cottage, was a bustling sparrow of a woman, who seemed convinced he was in danger of starvation and constantly offered him sandwiches, cakes and biscuits, for fear the packed meal Sally had provided was insufficient.

He sat in the right-hand bedroom and looked across the road at Palmer Stores. Phlegmatic by nature, for once he was suffering the need for success. A girl's life depended on that.

The extension phone rang.

'The sarge wants to know if anything's moving, Eric?' the caller asked.

'Bug—' He abruptly stopped. Sound travelled easily in the cottage. Since Miss Osborn watched a great deal of television, she would hear almost all swear words frequently, but he considered that some of those words, if spoken in her home, rather than on screen, would shock her. 'Nothing's stirring, sarge. What are they going to do if this doesn't work?'

'God knows, but they don't.'

'Can't stop thinking what it must be like for the girl. And her parents.'

'Can anyone?'

'You are qualified to carry out forensic work at the scene of a crime?' Querry asked.

'I am, sir,' PC Harbutt answered.

'On the eighth of November, were you and others called to Abbey Building, in Flexford, to conduct a search following the death of Mr Donaldson?'

'I was.'

'Will you describe your work?'

'We started—'

'We?'

'Members of the forensic team, sir.'

'Thank you. Please continue.'

'We first searched downstairs. The outside wooden door, which gave access to the passageway leading to High Street, was very solidly built. We noted that the bulb that illuminated the external door had been recently smashed; shards of glass lay scattered in the area beneath the light fixing. We then turned our attention to the door itself. On the outside

– that is, facing the passage – at a height of four feet eight inches, were faint marks.'

'You will be handed a photograph. Will you look at it and tell us if that shows the marks you have just mentioned?'

Photographs were handed to the judge, witness and jury.

Querry said, 'Please tell the court if these marks suggested anything to you.'

'I judged they showed considerable force had been applied to the door once it had been partially opened.'

'It is difficult to discern any marks in this photograph,' the judge observed.

'They are very faint, My Lord, and have not reproduced well, but the witness testifies he observed them,' Querry said.

The judge spoke to the witness. 'You have very good eyesight?'

'Just normal, I think, My Lord.'

'Very well.'

Querry resumed his examination. 'Did you reach any conclusion as to how the marks were impressed?'

'With considerable force.'

'Can you suggest the nature of that force?'

'It has to be a presumption.'

'Please presume.'

'A person used their shoulder in the form of a battering ram.'

'You have said at what height these marks were. Can you say, if a shoulder impressed them, what height the intruder was?'

'I was told by an expert in anthropometry standards that the person was approximately five feet nine to ten inches.'

'Please continue with the details of your search.'

'On the floorboards at the point where the victim's head had lain were stains. Part of the floorboard was removed and sent to the laboratory. The stains were found to be blood from the victim. By where the dog had been found were further stains. These were found not to be of human origin, but to have come from the dead dog.'

'Will you look at exhibits five and six?'

Two small squares of wood, pale on one side, and darkened by wear and age on the other, in plastic exhibit bags, were handed to the witness.

'Is that your signature on the identification labels?'

'It is.'

'Do you confirm these are the pieces of wood removed from the building?'

'I do.'

'What did you do next?'

'I examined the lock on the inner door, which gave access to the jewellery shop. This showed no evidence of there having been an attempt to force it. I moved upstairs. I found no evidence of criminal activity.'

'Thank you.'

Querry sat, Brooke stood. Two figures appearing or disappearing out of a model house, now not representing sun or rain, but guilt or innocence.

'Constable Harbutt, what were you told before you began your search?'

'I was given a normal résumé of the known facts, sir.'

'And were offered assumptions as well?'

'No, sir.'

'Were you not informed that the victim was very aware of the need for strict security and therefore the outside door must have been unbarred, unlocked and partially open for the assailant to gain admission, and also that it was presumed he had used his shoulder to slam the door fully open?'

'I was merely informed that there were no signs of forced entry, other than a smashed lightbulb.'

'Then it was logical to suppose the intruder gained entry very quickly. And the easiest method of doing so was, the moment the door was unlocked, to ram it open. You were expecting signs of contact on the outside of the door before you examined it, were you not?'

'I was expecting nothing. It is my job to search for signs of contact, whatever is said or not said.'

'But not to find them because you expect to do so.'

'That was not the case.'

'His Lordship asked if you had very good eyesight. Is it sufficiently keen to enable you to observe distinctly the marks on the photograph you have been given?'

'If I concentrate, yes.'

'Because you are convinced they are there. But anyone

without your unusual eyesight who has not been told they are there would, I suggest, fail to note them on the photograph.'

'I have explained, sir, that the photograph shows them less clearly than they could be observed on the door.'

'We have to take your word that that which is almost invisible to us is very visible to you. You have said you searched upstairs and found nothing of consequence. Even your acute eyesight failed to discern anything to suggest the murderer had gone up there?'

'I saw nothing.'

Brooke sat.

Scientists from the forensic laboratory were called and gave evidence that the stains on the two pieces of wood were respectively of human and canine blood, and that the human blood was from the deceased, the canine blood from the dog.

The court was adjourned.

EIGHTEEN

Drury rang Mallorca.

'Wendy's becoming rather difficult,' Diana said.

'Why's that?'

'The weather's become poorer, so there's no playing on the beach and she's bored and missing school.'

'Isn't time off school usually a reason for rejoicing?'

'She's remembered Jill's birthday party is next Saturday and, in her mind, the party's becoming ever more grand. Another thing. The season's ended and the owner is probably closing down until the spring. It means we'll have to find somewhere else to stay, and most of the other hotels are also closing.'

'Sorry to hear life's becoming less pleasant. Could you buck Wendy up by giving her a party?'

'All the English children who were here on holiday have returned home, and where do I find some local children who would like to attend a party given by someone they don't know and whom they can't understand?'

'A bad suggestion. My mind's not on the ball.'

'The police aren't any nearer finding the kidnapped girl?'

'Not as far as I know, and I'm sure I would have heard if they were.'

'You haven't found out?'

He had been too bitterly concerned with the future.

'I've finished bitching,' Diana said.

'Didn't realize you had been.'

'Liar. How's Audrey?'

'Very Audreyish. Still giving me hell for having moved back here.'

'My father always said she was a born sergeant-major. Is Basil fit?'

'And no doubt making money hand over fist.'

'Such a shame they can't have children.'

'Maybe fortunate for the potential kids. She'd have them square-bashing as soon as they could walk.'

'Steve . . . When will it all be over?'

'Before long.'

'How long is before long?'

'At a guess, I'll be called before adjournment on Friday evening.'

'I wish I was there to give you support.'

'Being able to talk to you is the next best thing.'

'I hope you really mean that. I'd better go – Wendy is beginning to sound off.'

'So I can hear. Tell her I'll have words with her if she upsets you and doesn't do as you say.'

'A threat from her teddy bear would carry more weight.'

They said goodbye, neither expressing the desire with which they longed to be together once more.

Ingham was called in late on Friday afternoon. The preliminary questions were soon completed, despite Querry putting them at unnecessary length.

'You were involved in the investigation from the start?'

'Yes, sir.'

'Initially, was it suspected or known who might be guilty of the murder?'

'I don't think so.'

'No mention of a possible culprit was voiced?'

'Not to my knowledge.'

'When was such a name first mooted?'

'A week or so after Mr Donaldson's death.'

'Are you able to tell the court who provided the possible name?'

'It was me.'

'What were the circumstances in which you were able to do this?'

'I was at home and chanced to pick up an old copy of a newspaper—'

'Of what name?'

'The *Drigg Gazette*.'

'You had bought a copy?'

'No, sir. My wife is regularly sent it by her mother, who lives in the Lake District.'

'Is this for any particular reason?'

'She was born and grew up in that area and has always remained very attached to it.'

'Do you regularly read the copy she receives?'

'No.'

'Why is that?'

'I don't really enjoy it. One needs to know the district and at least some of the people who live there to find it really interesting.'

'What did you read in the *Drigg Gazette* that you found to be of consequence?'

Ingham was about to answer when the judge spoke. 'Constable, you will not mention any name and you will not mention any detail that is not of immediate concern to this case.'

'No, My Lord.'

'Please tell the court the gist of what you read,' Querry said, 'remembering very clearly what his lordship has just said to you.'

'There was the report of a trial in which a man had been posing as a police constable in uniform in order to gain entry into houses on the pretext of examining the standard of security in them. Later, having gained the knowledge, he robbed them.'

'Since this happened up north, why should the information have interested you?'

'It had been suggested that the intruder had gained entry into Abbey Building by some subterfuge. I wondered if perhaps he had posed as a detective in a similar fashion.'

'Thank you.'

Brooke stood. The laws of evidence, the rule that no reference to a previous conviction was normally admissible, and the judge's warning, were all in his favour. 'Constable, is it correct that, having read the article in the *Drigg Gazette*, it became your contention that, in the circumstances of the murder of Mr Donaldson, the murderer had disguised himself as a police constable?'

'Not exactly. There were many objections to that theory.'

'Then what did you propound?'

'That he named himself a member of the CID, since then he could have worn civilian clothes and these would not have aroused unusual interest; equally, had he not done so, Mr Drury would surely have noticed the man who knocked him over was in uniform.'

'Did you put forward your theory to anyone?'

'To Sergeant Frenley.'

'Did anything in the article, apart from that which you mentioned, substantiate your theory?'

'Not directly, sir.'

'What about indirectly?'

The cross-examination continued, with Brooke trying to make the witness give inadmissible evidence, and Ingham struggling not to do so, since then the trial might be compromised.

On the television, the presenter's final observation was that the question was when, not if, a large meteor would strike the earth and annihilate millions of humans.

Ingham, trying to speak lightly, said, 'Two weeks ago we were all going to die from the heat of global warming. Last week it was from a super volcano. Our outlook is bleak!'

Jane made no comment. She was smoking. Once a regular, if light, smoker, she had given up the habit when the health warnings had become stark. She had resumed after he had questioned her about her relationship with Star.

He stood. 'I've had a tough day, so I'm for bed.'

'Joe,' she said sharply, 'I want to know something. I watched the news at six. There was a long report about your case.'

'Not surprising. I was approached by a TV crew, who wanted to know what I could tell them. I said I'd be hanged, drawn and quartered if I opened my mouth.'

'The commentator remarked that in court you had said something you'd read in the *Drigg Gazette* was important.'

'That's right.'

'Was it that which made you blame yourself so bitterly for having read the article?'

'If I hadn't told the sarge about it, there'd have been no reason to suspect Fitch and the girl would not have been snatched.'

'Normally, you never bother to read the paper. So why did you?'

'I . . . I'd just made a despicable fool of myself. I had to do something to try to calm my thoughts and hoped reading would help. It didn't, of course.'

'Is the girl going to be found?'

'I hope and pray, but . . .'

'If she isn't found in time, are you going to hold yourself responsible for what happens to her?'

'Not directly, but . . .'

'What?'

'Indirectly, yes.'

'It's because I was so upset, so shocked by your suspicions, so viciously unkind to you, that you read that bit in the *Gazette*. If I hadn't been so hurt, hadn't said and done what I did, you would never have read it. Then you couldn't have done anything that resulted in her being kidnapped. We're both responsible, yet you were just doing your job, while I was being a stupid bitch.'

'I had no right or reason to say what I did to you.'

'Sometimes right and wrong don't matter. Joe, we've been apart too long . . . I need you.'

He thought her logic faulty, was grateful it was. He crossed to where she sat, settled by her side, drew her against himself.

As he ate a large slice of sponge cake, liberally covered with whipped cream, PC Erwin accepted that the nature of perfection meant it could enjoy only a limited existence. A long shift that was spent staring across a road at a shop front soon became total boredom; and that was despite the goodies and sometimes slanderous chatter of Miss Osborn.

His mobile rang.

'Still nothing, Eric?'

'Less than nothing,' he answered.

'Beginning to look like a dead duck. But the sarge says to keep wide-eyed because it looks like there'll be movement very soon.'

'He's been saying that regularly since I started here. If you ask me, the villains are buying their grub and booze somewhere else and we aren't going to see as much of them as their shadows.'

'You're a mournful bastard!'

'So would you be if for a whole shift you had nothing to do but sit and look.'

'Too stupid to know when you're in the fifty-pound seats.'

NINETEEN

Drury walked to the end of the hall and back again. Pacing the bridge of the Titanic as she sailed towards the iceberg.

There was a call. 'Mr Steven Drury. Mr Steven Drury.'

He walked towards the courtroom doors and passed the woman whose voice he had been asked to listen to outside the grubby terrace house. She was dressed with much display and no taste.

The view from the witness box offered a different setting of a courtroom from the one with which he was familiar. The jury, now the harbinger of his future, were opposite him. To his right, Mr Justice Horricks was not a man to be humoured and persuaded, but a potential enemy. To his left, determined to steer him into victory for justice, Querry, overweight, a noted bon viveur with an incompetently concealed desire for promotion to the bench.

Drury placed his hand on the bible and took the oath.

Querry stood, took his customary time to sort through some papers before looking up. 'You are Steven Drury, you live at Parkside, Frainford, and are a barrister by profession?'

'That is correct.'

'On Monday, the eighth of November, were you dining with friends who live near to High Street, Flexford?'

'I was.'

'At what time did you leave your friends?'

'Around half past midnight.'

'Will you tell the court what occurred after you left?'

'I walked to where my car was parked.'

'Where was that?'

'In the small car park behind Sainsbury's supermarket.'

'Did you reach your car?'

'As I turned into the car park, someone crashed into me and knocked me to the ground.'

'Had you heard the person before the collision?'

'Not to be aware of his approach.'

'I am not certain what you mean?'

'I may have heard him, but did not consciously note that fact.'

'Were you shocked by this sudden event?'

'I was.'

'Were you also confused by it?'

'I think I must have been.'

Querry, surprised by the answer, hastily said, 'As one would expect. Nevertheless, you were able to express yourself in a vigorous manner?'

'I did not hear the witness say that,' the judge remarked sardonically.

'As your lordship pleases.' Querry addressed Drury: 'How did you react to events?'

'Once I was able to, I shouted angrily.'

'What effect did that have?'

'I was struck on the head.'

'Did that cause you to lose consciousness?'

'Probably momentarily.'

Querry leaned forward and spoke to his instructing solicitor. The latter picked up a sheet of paper and passed it back. Querry read briefly, then said, 'Will you tell the court what happened after you were struck on the head?'

'I was kicked in the side.'

'Very unfortunate. How would you describe the lighting in the car park?'

'Sufficient to determine form, but little or no detail.'

To Querry, this further difference from the original testimony at committal proceedings confirmed that the witness was – as known in the profession – a runner. 'What did your assailant do after he had kicked you?'

'Crossed to the other car in the car park.'

'The light was sufficient for you to observe that?'

'Yes. But not in detail.'

'What did he do when he reached the second car?'

'He opened the driving door and the interior light came on.'

'Was his face visible?'

'In part.'

'What do you mean by that?'

'He wore a hat and the collar of his mackintosh was turned up; because of the angle of face to light, only a small part of his visible face was illuminated.'

'But that was sufficiently clear for you to identify him at a later date?'

'Yes. Only . . .'

'What?'

'He climbed into the car very quickly, and the light immediately went out, so I had only a brief glimpse of the part of his face.'

'Nevertheless, you identified him from a photograph and at an identity parade?'

'Yes.'

'Do you now see in this courtroom the man you identified as having bowled you over, hit and kicked you?'

'Yes. I think so . . . Yes.'

'Who is that person?'

'The accused.'

Deciding further questioning could only weaken his case further, Querry sat.

The court adjourned. The judge left the bench, the courtroom slowly cleared. Querry gathered his papers together into a neat bundle, secured them with the white tape with which they had originally been tied, and made his way to the changing room. As he put his wig into a wig box, Brooke entered, said, 'Drury has about handed the case to the defence! Presumably he knew what he was doing.'

'Just as aware as you and I,' Querry said bitterly. He put his gown into his red bag.

'I've heard the whisper that the Stone girl was kidnapped in order to make him change his evidence. If so, it's difficult to blame him.'

'As a human being, yes. As a lawyer, no.'

Drury left his car, went around Parkside Farm to the front door, unlocked it, and entered. He poured himself a whisky, before walking into the sitting room and sitting on one of the two easy chairs by the side of the inglenook fireplace.

He had reached a decision after days of mental turmoil; he now faced the consequences of the decision on his personal as well as his professional life. He had entered the witness box, given his testimony, braced himself for the examination, and the court had adjourned. Since it was Friday, ahead of him was a weekend of bitterness.

PC Erwin looked at his watch. Whatever anyone said, time *could* stand still. Two hours still to go before the end of his shift. Two hours before he could return home, where Sally would probably greet him with, 'Hullo! Do I know you?' in a semi-humorous, semi-complaining comment on his working hours.

One car drew away from Palmer Stores, another took its place. The rhythm of boredom. This one was a battered Peugeot, no doubt owned by a farmer who complained that the poverty of farming had forced him to leave his Bentley in the garage.

The buzzer sounded. For several seconds, he was too surprised to move, then he hurriedly picked up the mobile and dialled HQ.

'Flexford county—'

'It's Eric. Visitor's arrived.'

'Car registration number?'

He gave it. The call over, he picked up the camera, which Frenley had handed to him with the terse comment that it was so simple, a child could use it, so if he made a b.u. of the photos, he'd spend a month on night duty. He took two shots of the passenger when the man was between the car and store, and one of the driver, even though the image would probably be too indistinct to be of any use.

He brought the tracker unit out of its box; it was small and mud-coloured, with three square sides and one slightly curved side, which provided an optional setting under a wheel arch. Too aware of how much rested on his success, he left the house, a borrowed shopping-bag in his left hand. As he approached the car, the driver looked briefly at him, then back at the outside shop-door, through the glass top half of which his companion was visible.

The underneath of the nearside wheel arch was dirty, but not sufficiently so to prevent the magnetized unit gaining a firm fix. As he bent and then stood upright, there was a shout from the front of the car. 'What's the problem?'

The driving window had been wound down, the driver, head turned, was staring at him, expression rough. Erwin walked up. 'What's that, mate?'

'What's so interesting about the car?'

'There was a piece of glass on the road. If you'd backed, you'd have gone over it and likely had a puncture.'

'Where's the glass?'

'I ate it. I was doing my good deed for the day. Next time, I won't bloody bother.'

'Sorry, mate, no bile intended.'

'None taken.'

It had been a narrow escape. He went into the shop. The car's passenger stood by the counter, on which were two cardboard boxes. He looked briefly at Erwin without interest.

'We'll do our very best,' Jenkins assured him.

'Don't need to be a genius to get it, do you?'

'It depends on the distributors. I'll tell them it's urgent and it should be here tomorrow. If you'd like to give me your phone number, I can tell you the moment it arrives.'

'I'll come back.'

Jenkins eased a bag of sugar into the second box. 'That's the last thing.'

'How much?'

'I'll just make certain—'

'Talk numbers.'

Jenkins checked the till's read-out. 'Seventy-six pounds and forty-three pence.'

The passenger put two fifty-pound notes on the counter, picked up one box and walked towards the door.

'I'll bring the other one out.'

'I'll come back.'

Jenkins activated the till, put the change on the counter by the second box, and then spoke to Erwin, giving no indication of recognizing him. 'Can I help you?'

Miss Osborn had remarked how much she liked cheddar cheese. 'Do you have some strong cheddar?'

'Certainly. And I can recommend it.'

'I'd like a pound.'

'If you don't mind waiting until I've given the other gentleman his change?'

'Of course not.'

The passenger returned, put the change without counting it into a trouser pocket, picked up the second box, and then left.

'He seems a bit on the sharp side,' Erwin commented.

Jenkins used a wire-cutter to slice a triangle out of the half cheddar. 'Not as friendly as many.'

'Do you know where he's staying?'

'I've only seen him the once before, and then he said less than he did now.' He put the cheese on scales. 'It's three ounces over the pound. Does that matter?'

'No . . . From the sound of things, he's been left short of something?'

'Whisky. I ordered it days ago and it's never arrived. People are becoming less and less dependable.'

Erwin returned to the cottage, gave Miss Osborn the cheese, thanked her for her kindness, and said he had never before tasted such wonderful sandwiches and cakes as she made: praise that delighted her even more than the cheese.

He drove to divisional HQ.

'Been on holiday like they tell me?' the duty sergeant asked.

'Days staring at a shop front and not a grain of sand or the sea in sight.'

'Any luck?'

'It's on.'

'Thank God for that! The inspector says to get up to him so quick that your shoes catch fire.'

Carren had been working at his computer. 'Well?'

'Two men in the car, sir.'

'Could you identify either?'

'No. But as I mentioned on the blower, I got photos. The tracker unit's in place.'

'You were undetected?'

'The passenger went into the shop, the driver remained in the car. He must have caught sight of me in one of the car's mirrors as I placed the tracker and demanded to know what I was doing. Said I'd picked up a piece of glass to stop him running over it and getting a puncture. Seemed to satisfy him.'

'What did they get in Palmer Stores?'

'A load of food, but no whisky because there wasn't any in stock.'

'As arranged.'

'How's that, sir?'

'He'll be back, and the more strings to the bow, the better.'

'You've been asking for identification on a grey Peugeot,' a PC in Vehicles said on the phone.

'Spot on,' Merriman answered.

'Nicked near Clapham Common. The owner couldn't understand why, since it was almost a wreck.'

'So who'd bother to look at it twice?'

Frenley went into the small room at the end of the corridor, normally filled with rubbish, now occupied by a civilian who sat in front of two visual display units and a pile of electronic equipment. 'How's it going?' he asked anxiously.

'Went dead a couple of minutes ago as it was entering South Allingdon.'

'The unit's fallen off?'

'If it had, it would still be operating. Just one more electronic glitch.'

'What are the chances of getting it going again?'

'Doing my best, but I'd be a sight more optimistic if there was a fifty-fifty chance of succeeding.'

'Things always go wrong when they're most bloody wanted.'

Frenley went along to the DI's office to break the bad news.

'We have a target?' Carren asked.

'The unit went dead outside South Allingdon.'

Carren swore. 'Is the operator going to get it back online?'

'He doesn't sound hopeful.'

Carren saw himself as much more a co-ordinator of the unit than a dictator, so before taking any decision, he called a conference at which rank would play no part. He spoke to those seated around the table. 'As you've probably already learned, the tracker unit has failed. On the facts as we have them, the course of events is clear. If Drury lies in court, as it seems he will when under cross-examination, Fitch will be found not guilty. This means Rose Stone is no longer of any use and, since she will be able to identify at least one of her kidnappers, she will be murdered. If Drury steps back at the last moment and does not lie, she'll still be murdered.

'With any luck – and we need it – the villains will soon return to the store for the whisky they were unable to buy on the last visit. So how do we take advantage of this?'

Merriman finally spoke. 'Lightning doesn't strike twice, so we could get a second tracker unit, which must work this time, and it's fixed on the car when they turn up to collect the booze.'

'Lightning has been known to strike the same person twice on a surprising number of occasions,' Carren said.

'We could ask the manufacturers to test a new unit until they're certain it can't fail.'

'Like any manufacturer, they'll swear the failure wasn't their fault. They'll say the unit was found and destroyed, for example. We need an idea that doesn't depend on electronics, that can't be ruined by something out of our control.'

'Bit of a tall order,' Frenley observed.

'Which is why we're here to find it.'

A couple of minutes passed before Park said, 'Maybe we could get them to take us to where she's being held.'

'But for one slight problem,' Carren said sarcastically. 'No doubt you can explain how that problem can be resolved.'

Park explained.

'You're out of your mind,' Frenley said angrily.

Carren reached up to scratch his head, needed to reset his toupee when he'd finished. 'They do say there's no problem that cannot be solved by laughter, bribery, or murder. I think self-destruction should be added to that list.'

Carren dialled county HQ, spoke to Moss. 'The tracker unit was successfully planted, sir, but on the journey it went dead. Every effort is being made to reactivate it, but so far without success.'

Moss swore.

'Hoping the kidnappers would be heavy boozers, and being

pessimistic enough to consider tracker trouble, I had arranged for Jenkins to say he was out of whisky, but would have it in tomorrow. Obviously, they may go into a town and buy what they want there, but we have to hope they'll be maintaining as low a profile as possible and return to the store.'

'Do you intend to plant a second tracker-unit?'

'This will be our last chance and I'd rather not tempt fate.'

'Then what do you propose?'

'I think, sir, it would be best if you do not know.'

'You expect me to accept that?'

'As the girl's life is at risk, I hope you will, sir.'

The line went dead.

Drury poured himself another drink. He could not escape, could not bind himself to a mast or still his hearing, he had to accept one or other fate.

On Saturday, no one stopped at Palmer Stores to demand if the whisky had arrived. The shop closed at eight, did not open on a Sunday.

TWENTY

Monday brought total cloud cover, drizzle, and a strong wind; the forecast was for steady rain. The weather matched Drury's mood as he stepped into the witness box.

'You are still on oath.'

Brooke rose to cross-examine, very conscious of the fact that since this was a high-profile case, gaining considerable media coverage, here was a chance to bring his name to the notice of many solicitors. 'Mr Drury, you have given evidence that on the evening of the eighth of November, you had dinner with friends in Flexford. 'Did you have a drink before the meal?'

'Yes.'

'What did you drink?'

'I think it was a gin and tonic.'

'How many drinks did you have before the meal?'

'One.'

'How many guests were there at dinner?'

'There were no others.'

'Did you have wine during the meal?'

'Yes.'

'Can you remember how many bottles of wine were opened?'

'One.'

'Was a liqueur offered after the meal?'

'Yes.'

'What did you have?'

'Cognac.'

'It would seem you dined and wined well! When you left your friends, you walked to collect your car which was parked in the small car park at the back of Sainsbury's supermarket. Do you know if this is restricted to employees of that supermarket?'

'It is.'

'Do you have special permission to use it?'

'No.'

'Your parking there was illegal?'

'I think it would be more accurate to describe it as a minor trespass.'

'On your return to the car park, you were knocked down by someone running into you. You have said you may have been aware of his approach, but did not consciously take note of it. That would suggest your mind was not clear enough to do so.'

'My mind was quite clear. I think it is quite normal to hear something and yet take no note of it because one's mind is otherwise occupied.'

'By alcoholic fumes?'

'By wondering how my family, who are abroad, were.'

'Have you described the quality of the light in the car park as sufficient to determine form, but little detail?'

'I cannot remember my exact words, but that is what I meant.'

'The constable who discovered you on the ground initially thought you were drunk and was only able to judge you were injured when you groaned and he switched on a torch to examine you further. Clearly, the light was too poor to make out any detail, even though he was standing next to you. You had been knocked to the ground, struck on the head, briefly lost consciousness, kicked in the side. One would imagine that, at the very least, you were mentally confused. Were you so?'

'To an extent, I think I must have been.'

'To what extent?'

'I cannot truthfully judge.'

'The man who knocked you down crossed to his car. During this time, were you able to observe his face?'

'No.'

'But you claim to have done so later?'

'When he opened the car's driving door and the interior light came on.'

'I think you have said that part, perhaps a large part, of his face was concealed by his hat and collar?'

'Yes.'

'And that your view of his face was further lessened by its angle with the light?'

'Yes.'

'You were able to observe only *part* of what was already a partially obscured face?'

'Yes.'

'Remind the court as to whether he was wearing an overcoat or a mackintosh.'

'I think it was a mackintosh.'

'That is what you have said in the past, but you now sound doubtful.'

'It was difficult to be certain.'

'Although the shapes of the two are markedly different, you now say you were unable to distinguish which was his outer garment?'

'Yes.'

'You would call it a question of outline, not detail?'

Drury did not answer.

'Detail becomes less visible as distance increases. When the man opened the car door and the light came on, was he as far from you as was possible in that car park?'

'I suppose so.'

'You remember so little, you cannot judge?'

'The place appears square. Since I do not know if that is fact, it might be slightly oblong in which case he might have been further away.'

'Was the interior light of the car bright?'

'Not particularly.'

'Would you describe the man's face as being strongly illuminated?'

'I would not.'

'Were there shadows across it, cast by parts of the car?'

'That's possible.'

'You cannot remember?'

'No.'

'Was the car's interior light on for several minutes?'

'No.'

'For how long?'

'Perhaps ten or fifteen seconds.'

'So would it not be reasonable to say that when someone

recently and grievously assaulted, who is dazed and lying on the ground, briefly looks up at an angle at a face largely obscured and fragmented by shadow, he is unlikely to observe an error-free mental picture of his assailant?'

'I can only repeat what I saw.'

'It is what you are *not* saying that interests me. For instance, why, when clearly you must have been uncertain as to the detailed appearance of the man by the car, did you at a later date claim to be able to identify him beyond question?'

'I never said that.'

'Were you not shown a number of photographs and, from these, picked out one that you identified as being of the accused?'

'Yes.'

'Then it is difficult to understand your denial.'

'I thought the photo was of the man I saw by the car.'

'We have heard evidence that far from expressing even slight doubt; you were certain of your identification.'

'At the time . . .'

'Yes?'

'I was certain.'

'And now you are not?'

Drury was silent.

The judge said, 'The court will adjourn for an hour in order for the witness to consider his evidence.'

PC Erwin's thoughts were bleak. He had been born under an unlucky star. He was back in the small front bedroom in Miss Osborn's cottage, staring across the road at the front of Palmer Stores. Perhaps he would be doing so until the end of his career.

The battered grey Peugeot braked to a stop in front of the shop. Erwin's sense of tension was instant. He watched one man leave the car and go into the shop.

The buzzer sounded.

He called on the mobile: 'Contact! Contact!'

One minute passed. Then another. 'Get the sodding thing moving!' he said, with angry excitement.

Miss Osborn opened the door; she held a plate on which were three scones. 'Is something wrong?'

'Sorry, Miss Osborn, didn't know you were near or I'd have said different.'

'I've just made these. I've buttered them and added strawberry jam, which I made myself, and some whipped cream from Old Basil's herd of Jerseys. I hope you'll like them.'

'I'm sure—' He stopped as he heard the first bellow of a tractor's exhaust. He crossed to the window as the tractor with lowered forklift came in sight. It approached the Peugeot with the majestic pace of an elephant. The forklift pushed into the front, smashing the radiator inwards and buckling the bonnet. As the tractor withdrew, the driving door of the incapacitated Peugeot was flung open and the driver stepped out on to the road, gesticulating and shouting; he was joined by a second man, who raced out of the shop.

'The tractor driver must be very careless,' Miss Osborn observed.

'It's probably the first time he's driven the tractor and he pulled the wrong lever.'

'What will the poor driver of the smashed car do?'

He wouldn't be driving anywhere, that was for sure.

'Since you're in the police . . .' She did not finish, evidently realizing she would seem to be criticizing him.

'It'll be an insurance problem, Miss Osborn, so there's no need for me to appear and complicate matters. May I have one of those scones?'

'They're all for you.'

He took one. 'When this is over, I'll be dreaming of all the wonderful goodies you've so kindly given me.'

Across the road, life was moving at a different tempo.

'You clumsy dickhead,' Lister shouted, as he stared at the immobilized car.

'Sorry, squire.' PC Hillard had taken considerable care to dress as his idea of a simple-minded farm labourer; he resembled someone in clothes rejected by a charity shop. 'You'll want the name of my insurance company.'

'What's the sodding use of that?'

'You'll be making a claim.'

Lister struggled to contain his fury. Since the car had been stolen, it had to be out of sight once more before there was any chance of the police becoming interested in it; he had to return to base quickly or the others – who were increasingly nervous, arguing over nothing, and viewing the girl as a wasting asset all the time she was untouched – might ruin everything . . .

'Worried about getting home, are you?' Hillard asked.

'You think I'm happy to stay here all sodding day?'

'The car still has four wheels.'

'And they'll turn their bloody selves?'

'I can hitch a rope and tow you to where you need to go.'

'When you can't drive for toffee?'

'It'll be no problem, like, since it wasn't my fault. The cat ran across the road, and your car was in the way when I avoided it.'

'Why didn't you squash it?'

'Belongs to Old Ma Younger. Dotes on it. It would have broken her heart to have it killed.'

'So it doesn't matter about my car?'

'I'll get you home.'

A coil of rope was secured to the tractor with bindertwine. Hillard cut the twine, secured the rope to car and tractor. 'How far is it, squire, and how do I get there?'

'I'll direct you. One sound on the horn, turn right, two, turn left.'

'Let's get moving.'

'We're not going anywhere before I get my stuff out of the shop.'

This time, the tracker unit, on the tractor, was working. In the room in divisional HQ, one VDU showed a map of nearby countryside and a small yellow dot, winking once a second, marked the course of the tractor and car.

Carren knew tension greater than any he had previously suffered. True, even if the unit again broke down, PC Hillard could report where he had been, but there was the possibility the car's driver, ever cautious, would demand the car was released away from the destination. Were that to happen, the area would have to be searched and news of this happening could so easily reach the kidnappers . . .

'It's stopped.'

He focussed on the screen. The dot of light was motionless. An ordnance map was open, and he marked on the spot indicated by the VDU. 'On the blower if there's movement.'

The operator nodded.

Carren hurried to the conference room where half a dozen PCs and a sergeant were waiting; he spread out the map on the table. 'Does anyone know this place?' he asked, as he indicated with a finger.

One of the PCs said, 'Brecton Farm, sir.'

'Describe it.'

'I only know it from the road. A modern house, medium size, built some time back to replace an old farmhouse that burned down. After the fire, the land was sold off. I've heard the place is owned by a woman in London who lets it to anyone prepared to pay a daft rent.'

'What's the surrounding land?'

'Grass fields. I think there's a small orchard between the house and the road.'

'What outbuildings?'

'A garage and some kind of shed.'

The public address system called the DI to the tracker room. Carren raced upstairs. The dot was once more moving – returning back along the road it had been on.

Seven minutes later, two cars left HQ. In the first was Carren, a sergeant and two PCs, one of whom was from an armed unit; in the second, four PCs. They drove out of town and along the motorway for three miles, turned right into country lanes. They stopped on a small rise, from which they had a clear view of Brecton Farm.

As the PC had said, the house was not large. Upstairs, clear-glass windows suggested three bedrooms, and the one with frosted glass, a bathroom. The right-hand window had drawn curtains. Downstairs, the front door was in the centre, and on either side was a window – dining room and sitting room? Kitchen, etc., would be to the rear of the building. The drive was bordered on one side by the garage and shed, on the other by rough grass; in front of the garage was the battered and useless Peugeot. There was room for the two cars to draw up alongside each other, reducing the time needed to disembark. Seconds were going to be vital.

Carren gave the order to go.

Speed, not stealth, became of concern. The cars went quickly down the sloping road and into the drive; they were fiercely braked and briefly slid along the gravel surface. The occupants of the first car raced around the house to cover the back; led by Carren, those in the second car made for the front door. The PC with a door-buster swung it; wood crunched. A second blow and it splintered; a third, the door slammed open.

There was a scream from upstairs. Carren led the way up and reached the landing as there was a second scream from the room to his right. The door was not locked and he flung it open.

Rose Stone was seated, a knife held against her throat by a small ferret-faced man who snarled, 'Keep back or I slice her.'

The armed PC withdrew his automatic, moved to gain a clearer view, and raised the gun.

Rose moaned, and the chair legs chattered on the floor as she trembled.

Each second became a minute before the knife was dropped to the ground.

TWENTY-ONE

T he court reconvened. The judge addressed Drury. His manner remained calm, his tone even, yet a sense of anger was clear.

'At the preliminary hearing, you gave evidence on oath that after you had been knocked to the ground, struck on the head, and kicked, you watched your assailant cross to the second car in the small car park. He opened the driving door and the inside light went on, which enabled you to observe his face sufficiently well enough, even if his hat and collar concealed part of his face, to be able to identify him when shown certain photographs.'

'Yes, My Lord.'

'You were asked to attend an identity parade. At that, you named the accused to be the man you had seen in the car park?'

'Yes.'

'At this parade, initially you were reminded you should be certain about your identification; you stated you were?'

'Yes.'

'Yet, in this court, you have expressed doubts as to those identifications you made?'

'Yes.'

'You will explain how this should be.'

'It . . . it is difficult, My Lord.'

'It is in your interest to overcome that difficulty.'

'I judged the authorities believed the man who killed the jeweller and knocked me to the ground must be represented in one of the photographs I was shown. One image was similar to my memory of the man in the car park.'

'Similar?'

'It was sufficiently like the man and since I had been shown a number of mugshots – that is, photographs of men who had been convicted in the past – I thought it had to be he.'

Amongst the lawyers, there were signs and sounds of aston-
ishment at this mention of a criminal past.

'You believed he must be guilty and therefore named him?'
the judge said.

Drury did not answer.

'It is deeply to be regretted that a member of the bar,
trusted to honour justice, should have knowingly pursued
injustice and ignored one of the fundamental rules of the
laws of evidence. You will not be surprised to know I shall
be forwarding details of your evidence to the appropriate
authorities.'

Captain Dreyfus, Drury thought. Sword broken, epaulettes
ripped off.

Brooke rose.

'Yes?' said the judge.

'My Lord, in view of the evidence we have just heard, I
submit that there is no case to answer. The prosecution has
provided no hard and fast evidence to connect the accused
with the murder of Mr Donaldson, other than the evidence
of the present witness . . .'

'There will be a retrial.'

It needed moral courage to walk into the changing room,
knowing any barrister there who had heard what had happened
would regard him with open contempt. The room was empty.
He disrobed with only his black thoughts as company.

As he walked towards the outside doors of the hall, a call
stopped him.

'Mr Drury.' Sergeant Frenley hurried around a group of
people to reach him. 'The guv'nor said to tell you Rose Stone
has been found, unharmed.'

He managed a genuine expression of relief. But the news
had arrived too late to prevent him from impeaching himself
and ruining his career.

In Interview Room No. 1 were Moss, who had been driven
down to Flexford at speed, Carren; Andrews, a solicitor; and
Mather, the knife-wielding, ferret-faced man arrested in Brecton
Farm.

'A woman phoned you and offered you the job?' Moss

asked, after the interview had been in progress for twenty-five minutes.

'Yes,' Mather answered sullenly.

'And you have no idea who she was?'

He didn't answer.

'It didn't strike you that a thousand pounds was such a large a sum for an unspecified job that you must be being asked to carry out an illegal act?'

'I thought the woman just needed help.'

'What form of help?'

'Didn't know.'

'You are medically trained?'

'No.'

'You are an engineer? A computer expert? A plumber?'

'No.'

'Do you possess any practical skills?'

Again, he did not answer.

'You are so unqualified, did it not make you wonder why you were being offered this money?'

'No.'

'You are often offered such commissions?'

'No.'

'What is the name of the woman who made this offer?'

'I've said, I don't know.'

'Why is that?'

'She didn't say on the phone.'

'How was the money going to reach you?'

'In the post.'

'In a bulging envelope that passed through the sorting office without being nicked by some light-fingered opportunist? You are an optimist. Your legal adviser will have explained to you the position in which you now find yourself, but perhaps you have not fully understood him. Miss Stone was kidnapped and held captive. A charge of kidnapping is one of the most serious on the books. You compounded the severity by threatening to kill her by holding a knife to her throat when the police found her.'

'No one said she'd been lifted.'

'You should have been more inquisitive.'

'I wouldn't of done it if they'd said.'

'Very careless of them. Looking at you, you're not young. By the time you come out, no one is going to offer you as much as a quid for doing "you know not what" to "you know not whom". Nasty outlook for you. Unless—' Moss stopped.

'What?' Mather demanded frantically.

'In some cases, when we tell the court that the accused has given us all the help he can provide, the judge often reduces the sentence he would have given.'

Mather was about to speak when Andrews forestalled him. 'If my client helps you in your investigation, in so far as it lies within his ability to do so, will you put in a good word for him?'

'You will be aware we can make no such promise.'

'You said you would.' Mather's voice was high.

'I said there was the chance. Name the person who promised you a thousand pounds and we may feel it suitable to explain the benefit of your admission.'

Mather began to chew the nail of his forefinger.

Moss spoke to Carren. 'Have we any idea who's likely to be trial judge for the next term?'

'I've heard it'll be Mr Justice Fetchley.'

'That's bad luck for anyone who comes up before him. Remember the villain who'd been nicking luxury cars and shipping them to Hungary?'

'I thought it was Poland.'

'Whichever, evidence was spotty and it took months to get him into the dock. Mr Justice Fetchley lectured him for twenty minutes over his lack of co-operation and handed out a maximum. Being dim, the defendant had been hoping for a light sentence.'

'You appear to be threatening my client,' Andrews said.

'Merely reminiscing,' Moss replied. 'If we were threatening, we would be far more specific.'

'What . . . d'you want?' Mather muttered.

'The name of the woman who paid you.'

'My client has continuously denied he was in any way implicated in the kidnapping,' Andrews said.

'Very optimistic, considering he was found with a knife at the victim's throat.'

'It was . . . ?' Mather stopped.

'Her name?' Moss demanded harshly, determined to crush any last resistance.

'Daisy.'

'Daisy who?'

'Can't say. Just Daisy.'

'Who's backing her?'

'Can't say.'

'You're not being as helpful as I hoped.'

'If I tell—'

'Afraid he'll cut your throat and we won't be turning up to stop him? If I give a name, don't respond or say it wasn't him and then you can swear on two bibles you never mentioned his name to us. Welland?'

No response.

'Harley?'

No response.

'Fitch?'

A nod.

'You can ask us in,' Carren said as he and Frenley stood outside the front door of Daisy Allen's house.

Her answer was several four-letter words.

'Then come back to the station while we find out whether you were an accessory before the fact to the kidnapping of Rose Stone.'

She went into the front room; they followed her.

'We've been having an interesting chat with a friend of yours – Barry Mather,' Carren said.

'Never heard of him.'

'Difficult to believe, when you offered him a thousand quid for a job.'

'Ain't offered anything to anyone.'

'Barry's been talking like a parrot that's swallowed a dictionary. About you getting in touch and offering him a thousand to guard Rose Stone after she'd been kidnapped.'

'You're talking shit.'

'I'm talking about you trying to help Dan Fitch escape a life sentence without remission.'

'Don't know any Fitch.'

'You're making our life difficult.'

'You think I'd help if you was drowning in a cesspit?'

'You could do yourself some good . . .'

Much of what Carren said was a repeat of what had been said to Mather. This time, it failed to gain as much as a hint of a confession.

Carren and Frenley returned to the CID car. Carren switched on the engine, did not immediately drive away. 'As tough as old boot leather. We've learned nothing to haul in Fitch again since Drury's evidence has been shot to hell. Or, for that much, to prevent Drury facing charges of perjury and trying to pervert the course of justice.'

TWENTY-TWO

Seated by the fireplace in the sitting room at Parkside Farm, Drury switched off the cordless receiver without having made the call. Diana had to know, yet for the moment he lacked the will to tell her. He finished the gin and tonic, accepted alcohol was not a solution, but left the room to pour himself another. The phone rang as he approached the corner cupboard in the hall.

'You've heard?' Audrey asked.

'They told me at the courthouse.'

'She's safe and, according to the news, physically unharmed.'

'That's what the police said.'

'How did they find her?'

'All they'd say was, they took a risk that paid off.'

'What happened in court? Did they know?'

'Not in time. I had to give my evidence before the news arrived. So I lied. The judge plainly expects me to be found guilty of perjury, disbarred, and detained at her majesty's pleasure.'

'Didn't you explain?'

'It would have been a waste of time.'

'Have you lost your senses? Or are you in one of your ridiculous moods and feel so guilty at having dishonoured your honourable profession that you must suffer consequences you don't have to?'

'I'm not that crassly stupid.'

'Then why?'

'If I'd tried to justify myself by explaining I was saving Rose Stone, I would have been asked, how could committing perjury and perverting justice accomplish that? The answer, to ensure Fitch was found neither guilty, nor not guilty. Impossible for any court to understand and accept.'

'Fitch *has* to be proved guilty now so that your lying was justified.'

'The police failed to uncover sufficient evidence, so it was only mine that brought him into the dock. Now that my evidence has been discounted, there is no way of proving his guilt.'

'The woman who gave him an alibi has to be made to admit the alibi is fraudulent, then when the case is retried and he is cross-examined, your evidence will prove his guilt.'

'Can you not understand my evidence has become worthless?'

'God, what a mess! You really think you'll be charged with perjury?'

'As things stand, it's as certain as nightfall.'

After a pause, she said, 'Is Diana returning tonight?'

'No.'

'When?'

'I don't know.'

'Surely you've told her what's happened and to get on to the first plane?'

'Why bring her back into this mess?'

'You think she'll thank you for not being at home to help at such an awful time?'

'I'd rather cope on my own.'

'Then you're a bloody fool.' She slammed down the receiver.

He drank.

The rain had cleared across the North Sea, the clouds were thinning, a frost had sharpened the air; briefly, January had lost some of its bleak dullness.

Drury, in the alcove opposite the front room at county HQ, stood as Carren approached.

'Morning, Mr Drury.' Carren held out his hand.

The duty sergeant was surprised by the friendliness of the greeting.

'Thanks for coming along, Mr Drury.'

'Surely, an unmissable invitation?' he said lightly.

'Would you come this way?'

They were joined by Frenley in the interview room. Carren switched on the recorder, gave date, time, and names.

'Mr Drury, on the evening of the eighth of November, did you leave your car in the private car park behind Sainsbury's supermarket in Flexford? Did you return there later that night after having spent the evening with friends? And on your return, as you entered the car park, did a man run into you with such force that he knocked you to the ground, then hit you over the head with a blunt instrument and kick you in the side?'

'Yes.'

'Were you at any time then, or later, able to observe his face?'

'When he opened the door of his car, the interior light illuminated his face sufficiently for me to note it.'

'Did you at a later date identify him as Daniel Fitch, both from a photograph and at an identity parade?'

'Yes, but at the time I did not know whom I was identifying.'

'Do you now confirm that identification?'

'Yes.'

'Do you wish in any way to amend your confirmation?'

'No.'

'Under direct examination, however, at the Crown Court, you suggested you were less than confident about your identification.'

'I may well have done.'

'Why?'

'In order to create the opportunity for Fitch to be found not guilty.'

'Was your evidence not true?'

'To the extent that I said I could not identify him beyond question, yes.'

'And under cross-examination, did you again cast doubt on your identification?'

'Yes.'

'At the trial, you gave evidence that, when you identified Fitch, you knew him to be a convicted criminal?'

'I did.'

'You were aware such evidence is only allowed in exceptional cases and this was not one such case?'

'Yes.'

'Was it a deliberate breach of the rules on evidence?'

'Yes.'

'You knowingly were trying to prevent the case continuing?'

'Yes.'

'Were you aware you were committing perjury?'

'I knew I had not told the truth.'

'Knowing you were doing so when on oath?'

'Yes.'

'Thank you, Mr Drury.'

'That's all? Then will you tell me something off the record?'

'I'm afraid I may not do that.'

'Never mind. Is there the chance of offering sufficient evidence to find Fitch guilty of murder at his next trial?'

'I intend to carry out a full review of all the evidence in order to find out if we have overlooked anything. Whatever the result, I fear your situation cannot change.'

'Then, accepting the obvious, my next appearance in court will be in the dock. They say one should enjoy every fresh experience. I don't think I will in this case.'

Carren closed down the recording with the time, switched off the machine. He spoke slowly. 'It is very seldom I regret having to carry out my duty, Mr Drury, but this is one occasion when I most certainly do.' He stood, and Frenley followed his example. 'If ever I find myself in a situation in any way comparable to the one in which you have been, I hope I will find a similar courage.'

Drury caught the train to Charing Cross, walked to the Temple, and went in to his chambers. As he entered the clerks' room, Rice hurriedly stood. 'Good morning, Mr Drury.'

He returned the greeting. 'Is Mr Ainsley in?'

'He is.'

'Anyone with him?'

Rice looked at his watch. 'Not for the next half hour, then he's seeing an instructing solicitor.'

'I won't keep him more than a couple of minutes.'

He left and went along the corridor to the main room, which was occupied by Ainsley, QC, head of chambers.

Ainsley, his long, thin face falsely suggesting a sharp, hard character, stood. 'Good to see you again, Steve.'

'I gather you've a client arriving soon, so I won't keep you.'

'There's no rush. Grab a seat.'

'I thought it would save any embarrassment if I came in and cancelled my membership of these chambers.'

Ainsley, now again seated, had the habit of resting his elbows on desk or table, raising his forearms and joining the tips of his fingers together, and then speaking over the triangle they formed. 'Why?'

'You've surely heard about my effort in court?'

'Of course. The news travelled faster than light.'

'Horricks made it very clear what he thought of me.'

'He was sanctimonious even before he made the bench.'

'Yesterday, the police questioned me. They were surprisingly sympathetic, but they had a job to do. I admitted I had lied on oath in court and knowingly disclosed the accused's previous record. The DPP will hold I be charged and tried; on my own admission, I am guilty. That means almost certainly a jail sentence and my disbarment. I either leave these chambers now, or when I am thrown out.'

'I understand you had good reason for your actions.'

'My evidence was vital to the prosecution's case. By making it obvious I was lying, by disclosing the man's record, I was forcing another trial, *which* would keep the girl alive.'

'Why?'

'Whether Fitch was found guilty or not guilty, Rose Stone would be murdered, since she could testify against her abductors.'

'You must have informed the police?'

'They did their damnedest to find her, but by the preliminary hearing, they had failed. Before the trial, I was sent a lock of her hair to remind me what would happen if I did not make certain Fitch was found not guilty. I had become her passport to hell. I only knew she had been rescued after I had already given my evidence.'

TWENTY-THREE

As Drury turned into the drive of Parkside Farm, a light was showing in the sitting room. The automatic switch appeared to have come on early. He walked around to the front door. The hall light was on, the front door was unlocked. He stepped inside. There was the sound of running feet, and Wendy reached him and demanded to be lifted for a hug.

'What, young lady, are you doing here?' he asked as he lowered her.

'Mummy said we had to come back because you were acting like a . . . Can't remember.'

'Imbecile,' Diana said as she stepped out of the sitting room.

Wendy had finally gone to bed. Diana had lit a log fire because even if the central heating was on, a drink beside an open fire was the epitome of a homecoming.

'Audrey should not have got in touch with you,' he said as he handed her a glass.

'So you have already remarked several times.'

'I told her, I didn't want you coming back to the mess.'

'Being a sensible woman, she ignored you.'

'Being an interfering sister.'

'Do you really think I wanted to remain over there when you were in trouble?'

'You did not know I was until she told you.'

'And thank goodness she did.'

'I hoped to spare you the worry.'

'I know that, my darling; and it makes me uncertain whether to kick you or kiss you.'

'Reduce the problem to a kiss.' He stood, went over to her chair and kissed her, before putting a log on the fire and returning to his seat.

'How bad are things?' she asked.

'Not very bright.'

'What does that mean?'

'I will be charged with perjury and with trying to pervert the course of justice.'

'But you lied in order to save a girl's life!'

'Because Fitch cannot be proved guilty, my reason for lying has no strength.'

'I don't know how anyone could think like that.'

'Lawyers enjoy the ability in abundance.'

She stared at the flames gathering around the freshly-placed log. 'What's going to happen?'

'Impossible to say right now.'

'How bad could it get?'

'Let's forget the future and enjoy your homecoming.'

Carren paced behind his desk, watched by Frenley.

'There has to be the evidence of guilt somewhere,' he said suddenly, as he came to a halt by the window. 'There's never contact without a trace!'

'So they tell us when it's not them who has to find the trace.'

'You've been through all the reports?'

'Read every word more than once, sir. Spoken to one of the laboratory staff, who was pissed off because he reckoned I was criticizing them for not doing their job properly. Talked to Sergeant Holmes, and he swears the forensic team couldn't have done a better job if they'd spent another couple of months in the building.'

'Daisy Allen. Break the alibi she's provided Fitch.'

'Might as well try to climb Everest in trainers.'

'Hardly helps when you're determined on failure.'

'Just facing facts, sir. From the beginning, she's laughed at us.'

'Park could have another shot at removing her smile.'

'With Fitch out of jail, you could hold a lighted candle under her feet until they were toasted and still she'll swear they were together all that evening.'

Carren stopped pacing and sat on the corner of his desk. 'We've always assumed she's lying. What if we accept she is telling the truth? Then Drury lied in court for a reason other than the one he gives.'

'We've been through this . . .'

'We'll go through it again. Has he been bribed by Fitch to lie?'

'How could that fit the known facts?'

'I'm damned if I know, but we haven't yet checked up on his bank accounts, or made a careful estimate of his recent spending – has he bought a new car, or a flat-screen television the size of a billiard table? Have he and his wife been staying at five-star hotels? What's his mobile-phone history? Has he been making calls to a contact of Fitch's?'

'You want us to pursue these enquiries?'

Carren spoke angrily. 'I know, it's crazy thinking. It's the goddamn frustration of knowing all we can do is check what has already been covered again and again.'

'Do we try the Allen woman?'

'You've suggested it's a waste of time.'

'Can't think of a better way to waste it, sir.'

'I don't believe it,' Daisy Allen said as she faced Park.

'It hasn't had cosmetic enlargement.'

'I'm bloody well—'

'Going to complain I'm harassing you? The charge sergeant will tell me that I should be so lucky.'

'What is it this sodding time?'

'How about playing "in pops the weasel"?'

'Sooner play with a dead rat.'

'Are you asking me in?'

She went to shut the door; he moved quickly to prevent her doing so. 'You need to hear what I have to say.'

'Like I need arsenic.'

'Don't you like the rustle of money?'

'You think you'd smell any better with a fifty in your hand?'

'I'd never insult you by offering to pay . . . There's a solid reward that'll make you smile.'

'What for?'

'Offer me a cup of tea and I'll tell you.'

After a while, she stepped back. 'Shall we chat upstairs?' he asked as he entered.

She went into the front room.

'How does the sound of ten fifties interest you?' he asked.

'Tells me you're on the take, like any other split.'

'All you have to say is maybe you did get some facts wrong and there's five centuries in your handbag.'

'You think I'd welsh for five hundred?'

'Is that what I said? I meant a thousand.'

'Shove it.'

'So wasteful. Let's make it a couple of grand, with no one asking if you've paid tax on it.'

'And have my throat cut before I'd spent a single quid?'

'You don't seem to understand that—'

'It's you, you stupid sod, who doesn't.'

'Listen to your uncle, who's not the one with bad breath and wandering fingers. Fitch knew Drury had seen him minutes after he'd topped the jeweller and could do him for a lifer. So he snatched Rose to persuade Drury to forget what he saw. An old-fashioned idea, but it worked. That is, until she was found and it was game, set, and match to the law. They've evidence to support identification of him as the murderer of old Donaldson, but he's still shouting his alibi. Go into court and give the same evidence as ever and you'll be turned inside out and then charged with trying to pervert the course of justice. So remember what really happened and you'll have money to spend when, with him inside on a lifer, he can't get near enough to see your throat, let alone cut it.'

'And you think he can't make things happen when he's inside?'

'We'll protect you.'

'Like you protected Gertie?'

'Who?'

'Bugger off.'

'You invited me in.'

'And now I'm inviting you out.'

'Your evidence can save an innocent girl.'

'Think I'm in the Jolly Drum Brigade?'

'He's married and has a kid. She's hardly had time to live. They'll suffer if you don't tell the truth.'

'Still don't understand if I can kick the bastard in the goolies, I'm laughing until I leak?'

Park returned to divisional HQ. He spoke to Frenley. 'Back from Daisy, sarge. It's a no-no, and I'm saying there's not a chance of getting her to admit the truth. Won't listen to bribery, threats, or an appeal to her better self.'

'I suppose it was worth a final try.'

Park began to leave, then checked the movement. 'Who's Gertie, and what happened to her?'

'Why ask me when you're the self-proclaimed expert?'

'When I told Daisy we'd look after her, she said, "Like you looked after Gertie?" and it wasn't being complimentary.'

'This Gertie was someone we were meant to be guarding?'

'That's how I took it.'

'The name doesn't ring any bells.' He stood. 'I'll tell the guv'nor about your talk with Daisy. Just as well the messenger doesn't get shot these days.'

'How's that?'

'Ask Google.'

Frenley went along the corridor to Carren's room. 'Just had Park back, sir. No luck with Daisy, despite all he tried; even appealed to her good nature.'

'We're getting nowhere very quickly.' He scratched a tickle under his toupee. 'How about some suggestions?'

'Can't offer any, sir.'

'Then it looks like a case going into deep freeze. Still, to use a detective's all-embracing excuse, we can't win them all.'

Frenley did not leave.

'Is there something more?'

'Does the name Gertie mean anything to you, sir?'

'Why the question?'

Frenley explained.

For some reason, Carren became silent.

Frenley waited, finally began to leave, and had reached the door when Carren said, 'Gertrude Williams.'

'What's her story?'

'Can't remember all the details. Goes a while back. She ratted

on a villain after she'd been promised police protection. Went
missing and wasn't found until she was a bag of bones in a
wood near Bradford. My wife's from there, which is why I
remember the case. If that's the right Gertie, why would Daisy
have remarked about her? Because there's a connection through
Fitch? Get hold of the facts.'

'Yes, sir.'

'If we can show Daisy has very good reason to know how
she'll end up if she snitches on Fitch, we can tell her it was
Gertie's own fault she was topped, and if she does as we tell
her she'll be OK, but she's heading to jail for non-disclosure
unless she starts playing ball.'

Diana stepped into the hall as Drury hung up his Barbour
jacket. 'Are you very wet?' she asked.

'It stopped raining soon after I started walking.'

'Did you go far?'

'Lower Rinderton.'

'There and back is the best part of five miles.'

'The exercise helps.'

'I wish—' She stopped. She spoke again, her voice touched
with despair. 'Why do we wish the past was different when
we know it can't be?'

'Human nature at its most illogical.'

'Are you going to have coffee?'

'And a large slice of cake, please. Where's Wendy?'

'Frieda's mother rang to say she'd heard we were back
and would Wendy like to go and have tea there. She and
Frieda are great friends, for the moment, so I ran her over.
She's to be fetched at seven, if you wouldn't mind?'

'Of course.'

'I'd go and enjoy a quick chat with Margot, but I must
prepare our meal.'

'Are we having something high-powered for supper?'

'I've asked Audrey to dinner.'

'You've what?'

'I'm not having you going on and on moaning because
she called me back without telling you.'

'Moaning?'

'Pathetically.'

'What are you cooking?'

'Leg of lamb and chocolate pudding.'

'At least part of the evening will be sweet.'

'If I didn't know you were *trying* to goad me, I'd be goaded.'

TWENTY-FOUR

Carren entered Frenley's room. 'Any joy with Gertie?'
'Just heard from Bradford, sir, and was about to come along and tell you. Some time back, Gertie Williams was living with Yates, a local villain. He was picked up in the flat of another woman and there was no argument about what he was doing there. Hearing this, Gertie blew the whistle under the promise of police protection and incriminated him. He was given five years. The sentence reduced by good behaviour; he came out early and found an opportunity to murder her. Earned him a lifer.'

'Nothing to do with Fitch?'

'No.'

Carren walked past the desk and stared out of the window. 'When I was a kid, I used to have to go to Sunday school. We were given the quote, "Let us do evil, then good may come." I couldn't understand the logic then and I still don't. Reverse it, though, and it does.'

'You're thinking of Drury?'

'Yes.'

Diana and Drury met Audrey and Basil in the hall. Wendy, supposedly asleep, greeted them from the top of the stairs.

'How's my favourite niece?' Audrey called out.

Her gaze was fixed on the small package in Audrey's right hand.

'Are you going to come down and give me a kiss?'

Wendy quickly descended.

'I've a present for you because you're looking so wonderfully fit.'

'Like the one you gave me before we went because I was looking so pale?'

There was brief laughter. They went into the sitting room. Wendy unwrapped her present, Drury fetched a bottle of Mumm in a cooling jacket and four flutes. He filled the glasses, handed the first to Audrey.

'Thanks, Steve,' she said. 'Now, aren't you glad I ignored your stupidity?'

'I suppose.'

'What a boorish response.'

'I, for one, am very, very glad,' Diana said. 'And I still cannot understand how my husband could have thought I ought to stay on the island.'

'If I admit to a total lack of understanding of the female mind, can the subject now be dropped?' Drury asked.

In the hall, Audrey had just put on her fur coat, which she chose to wear as often as possible to annoy the critics of the fur trade, when Timpson said, 'You're forgetting something.'

'Must be catching the fault from you,' she answered. 'What am I supposed to have forgotten?'

'The tie.'

'You said *you'd* bring it in.'

'The definition of a good husband is one who falsely accepts he is in the wrong,' he said. 'I forgot.'

'Is it still in the car?'

'Seems it must be, since in truth you forgot to bring it in.'

'Deuce?' Drury suggested.

'Deuced awkward woman,' Timpson suggested, with the freedom which came from a long and happy marriage. He went out.

Audrey said, 'Steve, you remember you were undressed in hospital and later the police came here and wanted all your clothes?'

'And you collected them and they held them for days.'

'Earlier, when I was waiting at the hospital to hear how you were, a nurse came out with you to say you could leave and she told me that when you'd dressed, she'd suggested you didn't wear your tie; she gave it to me instead. I rolled it up and shoved it in the pocket of the decrepit coat I'd put on in the panicky hurry to get to the hospital. Yesterday I had to do some housework—'

Drury interrupted her. 'Who explained how?'

Audrey spoke to Diana. 'Does he still go on like that all the time?'

'Not continuously, since I've managed to persuade him to accept how many years it was since he'd been at school.'

'Doesn't seem to have accepted as well as you thought. Anyway, I came across the tie and remembered why it was there. Basil is bringing it in for you.'

Timpson returned, handed Drury a plastic shopping bag in which was the rolled-up tie. 'We'll be on our way, after many thanks for a happy evening.'

Drury escorted them to their Jaguar, returned indoors.

'Ready for bed?' Diana asked.

'More than.'

'You did enjoy their coming here, didn't you?'

'I did. And I guess it's just possible I was wrong and Audrey was right to phone you in Mallorca and tell you what was happening.'

She hugged him. 'A rare admission!'

'Since it so seldom is necessary.'

She went upstairs; he made certain doors and windows were fast before he followed. She had begun to undress; he sat on the bed and stared at the Aubusson carpet.

'Steve, you've got that gone-away look.'

'Seeing the tie has lit up memories – being knocked to the ground, trying and failing to make sense of everything, the policeman asking me if my wife was at home and my wishing he'd clear off and leave me to suffer in silence . . . Funny how something as insignificant as a tie will stir up the memory.'

She unclipped her brassiere. 'Of course it can . . . Are you looking lost because you think it's a weakness to be upset by memories?'

'Amateur psychiatry by IM Wong?'

'As you've already proved tonight, at least your sense of humour hasn't changed.'

Carren braked to a halt alongside the garage. He stared through the windscreen at Parkside Farm. There might be no such thing as an ideal life, but to live in the English countryside, in a timber-framed house, was perhaps as near to it as one could hope to get. Yet what kind of a life did Drury face?

He walked around to the front door, rang the bell. Mrs Drury opened the door.

'Is Mr Drury at home?' he asked.

'He's just gone into Flexford, but should be back soon. Would you like to come in and wait?'

'If I may.' He stepped into the hall.

'Does your coming here mean more trouble?' she asked uneasily.

He prevaricated. 'Nothing fresh, Mrs Drury.'

'Would you like some coffee?'

'That would be very welcome.'

In the sitting room, there was a copy of *Country Life* by the chair on which he sat. He picked it up and played If-I-Was-A-Rich-Man as he decided which of the advertized properties he would buy. The château in Burgundy with its own vineyard; the castle in Scotland; the estate in England with Georgian mansion, six cottages, seven hundred and fifty acres of productive (agent-speak in financially depressed times) farmland and a hundred and ten acres of woodland, carefully parcelled to provide a shoot with notably high birds . . .

'I've put out some chocolate biscuits in case you might like them,' Diana said as she entered, carrying a tray which she put down on a table. She asked him to help himself. He ate and drank, uneasily aware this had taken on the ambience of a social visit, rather than one in which he would inform Drury he was to be charged with perjury.

'Do remind one of us to give you the tie,' she said.

What tie, and why should it be given to him? he vaguely wondered as he ate a second chocolate digestive.

In his office, Carren opened the plastic bag and brought out the tie Drury had given him, saying the forensic laboratory had not had the chance to examine it. He had not observed that since none of the other clothing had offered any evidence, this was unlikely to do so. It was of very good quality as one would expect, more regimental or old-school in colour and design than the modern rainbow style. He began to return it to the bag when the angle at which he was holding it enabled him to notice a small dark dot; as he studied it closely, he noticed others beyond, irregularly spaced. His wife liked poetry; Had Cortez stared with such wild surmise as he did now?

He hurried along to Frenley's room; it was empty. In the CID general room, Ingham, looking almost cheerful, was working at a computer.

'I need tissue paper,' Carren said.

'I'm sorry, sir?'

'Tissue paper. Don't you know what that is?'

'Yes, but . . .' Ingham stood. 'I'll try and find some.'

The stores cupboard held none. Park, whom he met along the corridor, wanted to know what needed to be wrapped with such delicacy; below, the duty sergeant said, 'You won't find any around here. What about paper handkerchiefs? Would they do the trick – whatever the trick is?'

'Have you some?'

'A box, seeing as I've a stinking cold and a nose running faster than Bannister ever managed.'

'Let's have it.'

'Hang on, it's personal, not stores.'

'I'll bring them back.'

'What's it for?'

'I don't know.'

'Par for the course for you lot.' He removed several paper handkerchiefs, which he put down on the counter before handing the box across.

Ingham returned to the DI's room. 'The best I can do, sir, unless you want me to go out and find a shop that stocks the stuff?'

'They'll do. Give me a hand to fix them around the tie.'

They interlaced handkerchiefs with the rolled-up tie.

'I want something to put this in so there can't be any chafing.'

'I've a small cardboard box, which should do.'

'Get it.'

When opened, the box emitted a strong scent.

'Yours?' Carren sarcastically asked.

'Only after-shave lotion, sir.'

'Made me think you were into perfume. Scrumple up the rest of the handkerchiefs so they keep the tie really secure.'

Ingham carried out the order. 'That won't move any way.'

'You'll be back on the beat if it does.' Carren carefully checked the holding paper. He shut the lid and found two rubber bands, which he secured around the box. 'Make out a movement note, then get this below and tell the duty sergeant it's to be delivered to the forensic laboratory right away. I'll give them the details.'

Ingham picked up the box. 'Is it to do with—' He stopped. Carren did not like his orders queried.

For once, there was no admonitory comment. 'I am hoping like hell that it is a loaded gun.'

Which did not answer the question Ingham had not asked. He left the room.

Carren phoned the laboratory. 'There's a tie on its way, which should be with you inside the hour. It was worn by Steven Drury on the night he was knocked over and assaulted, following the murder of Donaldson. On it are a few small, dark dots – there may be more, not readily visible – which could be dried blood. It might have come from Drury, but I'm hoping like hell it didn't.'

'We'll check it as soon as we can.'

'On arrival.'

'Inspector—'

'You've twice as much work as you can handle, so this will have to wait its turn? . . . You've nothing more important in hand, since a woman's safety and a man's freedom may rest on your report.'

'We'll start as soon as we get it. I'll phone the moment we have a result.'

Carren did not quickly return to the humdrum world of work; for a while, he stayed amongst the clouds of hope.

Wendy was in bed and, hopefully, asleep. They sat by the fire, Drury to the left, Diana to the right, their seats at an angle to give them a straightforward sight of the television set.

'Steve, are you enjoying this programme?' she asked.

'Not really.'

'Then let's switch it off.'

'Or try another channel?'

'There's a programme you want to watch?'
'There might be something worthwhile.'
'It's not like you to look for the sake of looking.'
'It dulls the brain.'
'Please switch off.'
He used the remote to do so.
'You're worried sick, aren't you?'
'Worried, but that's to be expected.'
'Until now, you've always been able to ride out a problem.'
'I suppose this one bucks a little.'
'What is the worst that can happen?'
'Why bother when it won't?'
'It's no good talking like that. I must know so that I am prepared for it.'
He was silent.
'Please tell me, love.'
'As things stand, I am going to be found guilty of perjury and, very probably, perversion of the law.'
'What will that mean to you?'
'As a barrister, it's my job to serve justice, not kick it in the teeth. Any plea in mitigation will raise sarcastic laughter.'
'Are you saying you could be sent to jail?'
'That has to be the probability. They'll need to make an example of me . . . . Christ! I shouldn't have married you to drag you into this mess.'
'However bad the future, I am forever glad you did marry me.' There was a brief silence, which she broke. 'Could it be for rather a long time?'
'Yes.'
'Then . . . What would happen afterwards?'
'On conviction, I'll be disbarred. Even if that was not inevitable, the trial will cause even more adverse publicity for me, and there won't be a solicitor in the country willing to brief me.'
'What would you do then?'
'In the more enlightened and less crowded prisons, inmates are taught a trade. I could learn to be a plumber. They have to pay super-tax. Or perhaps I'll go on the after-dinner speech trail, relating my experiences in prison, allowing the good to congratulate themselves on their virtues

and the sweet old ladies to enjoy brief contact with evil without being defiled.'

'I wish you wouldn't try to make light of it . . . We've always saved, but I don't suppose our savings will last very long with today's prices. If you can't earn . . . We won't be able to continue to live here, will we?'

'Something has to come our way.'

'I can't just hope, Steve. I must face facts, for all our sakes. If necessary, we'll sell and move to somewhere smaller. We can make do with one car. If you're out in it and I have to go to the village, I'll bicycle. Wendy would have to go to a state school . . .'

'You're making me feel I should fold up in order to release my life insurance.'

'If you die, only Wendy can give me reason to go on living.'

The laboratory assistant rang. 'Inspector Carren?'

'Speaking.'

'Preliminary tests show the spots on the tie were not human blood.'

Carren thanked the other, replaced the receiver, stared bleakly at nothing.

TWENTY-FIVE

D rury left the house and slowly walked towards the woods. One could accept that one faced the inevitable, and prepare to meet it, yet be unable to resign oneself to it. He loved the countryside – fields, thorn hedges, woods, birds, animals, the relative solitude, space, quiet. Life behind bars denied one all that and more. Without his earnings at the bar, Audrey would have to find work, bitterly regretting what this would mean for Wendy.

He reached the bourn, a small stream that dried up in summer, which ran between the slight bank of the field he was in and the steeper bank of the woods. A cynic said one never truly valued anything until deprived of it. He had seen the bourn countless times; now he studied the running water as if it were a noted trout stream.

He crossed and began to climb the slope. Halfway up, a cock pheasant exploded out of a clump of brambles and flew, zigzagging between the thirty-year-old growth of pollarded ash and chestnut trees and uncut, ancient oak trees. He watched it, a map of colour, climb above the trees and disappear. One the poachers had missed. He wished it continued freedom.

Frenley studied the unfinished duty list for the next month. He and Madge had been asked to stay with their elder son for a weekend. On their return, Madge would yet again refer to the table manners of their young grandson. 'It's a wonder he bothers to use a knife and fork and doesn't just throw what he doesn't want on to the floor like Henry the Fifth.' That time, he had not corrected her. Her occasional historical mistakes increased his affection for her.

The phone rang. He looked at his watch, hoping this was not going to be an introduction to something which would keep him at work until midnight instead of watching the telly with a glass of proper beer at his side, waiting for a solid meal, cooked by Madge. He lifted the receiver.

'Inspector Carren?'

'Sorry, he's away. Detective Sergeant Frenley speaking.'

'Forensic laboratory. We've a further report on the tie. The blood was canine and we have been able to match it against the blood from the dead dog at the side of Donaldson. I'm letting you know this late because the inspector was obviously in a rush to know the result.'

Frenley thanked the other, replaced the receiver, took a cigarette out of the pack in the top drawer of his desk, and lit it, careless that smoking was forbidden in the building. He needed to think calmly, not just race to the conclusion he wanted . . .

After dinner, Drury had walked from his friends to the car park. There, he had been bowled over. He had not left the car park until carried away in an ambulance. It was, therefore, impossible for him to have been in Donaldson's house after the dog had bled profusely. Then how could there be the dead dog's blood on his tie?

He had been attacked by Fitch in the car park. Earlier, Fitch had defended himself against the schnauzer in Donaldson's flat and had coshed it, probably continuing even after death because of wild anger. Inevitably, the cosh had become heavily tainted by the dog's blood. Moments later, the cosh had been used to silence Drury. That meant the cosh had been raised before it was brought down with as much force as possible. This arcing motion would have cast off some of the dog's blood, and drops of this had spattered Drury's tie . . .

He hurried to the DI's room. The movements' book showed Carren had earlier returned home. He dialled the other's home number, spoke to Mrs Carren. 'Sergeant Frenley speaking. May I speak to the inspector?'

'Must you? He's very tired,' she said sharply.

'It is important.'

'Very well.'

There was a pause before Carren said, 'Yes?'

'Sir, the laboratory has just reported that the blood on Drury's tie was the dog's.'

There was a silence which Carren finally broke. 'And there

is no way it could have got there unless it was Fitch who ran into Drury and attacked him.'

Carren stood in the sitting room at Parkside Farm.

'Are you sure?' Diana asked him, pleading for confirmation as she stared at her husband.

'We can now prove it must have been Fitch who assaulted your husband in the car park and that his identification of Fitch was correct.'

'But he . . . I mean, he denied he could be certain it was Fitch.'

'If he has not already done so, I am certain your husband will explain he is entitled to claim he was concerned with the fate of Rose Stone and therefore lacked the intent to lie when on oath.'

'But he did lie to save the girl.'

'Legal intent in this context is not the same as ordinary intent,' Drury said.

Carren spoke. 'I will be forwarding all the facts to the CPP. I think we may accept there will be no prosecution for perjury.'

'I wish to be prosecuted,' Drury said.

'Don't listen to him,' Diana said wildly. 'It's his crazy sense of humour. He thinks he's being funny,'

'No, sweet, I am being very serious. When I was lambasted in court by the judge, I became headline news even in the broadsheets. I need to erase that infamy.'

'I think you're talking nonsense.'

'Do *you*, inspector?'

'You place me in an invidious position, Mr Drury. I have to admit the idea can be regarded with some doubt, but it might also be considered a smart move.'

'You would make a good lawyer,' Diana said.

Mr Justice Cliff-Montague looked older than he was because of his heavily-lined face, and sterner than he wished to be thought because of his heavy, square jaw and very firm mouth. He had a quick intellectual, yet practical mind, disliked counsel who wasted time arguing legal points of little relevance, but which pleased their clients.

'Members of the jury,' he said, his tone warm and low-pitched, 'the accused is charged with perjury; for the purpose of this case, it may be defined as knowingly, and with intent, lying when on oath to tell the truth. You have heard him accept that this was so; that he was fully aware he was not telling the truth when he denied he could identify a certain person after having seen him in the light from the interior of a car. At an earlier hearing, he had sworn on oath he could so identify that certain person.

'You have heard Mr Drury explain he lied in order to try to save the life of a young woman who had been kidnapped. You have heard two members of the police force confirm he had been threatened that to give his evidence truthfully would result in her death; you have heard them testify he had received a lock of female hair which in his mind, and theirs, meant that if he did not lie in court, the young woman would be mutilated, raped and murdered. Yet it was also his belief and, once again, the police agreed with him, that if he did lie and the accused was found not guilty and was released, she would still suffer that fate because of the evidence against them that she could give. A seemingly impossible situation yet, with courageous self-sacrifice, he faced it and, despite knowingly perverting the court of justice, he made certain that she lived until she was rescued.

'There are exceptional occasions when a person may be justified in knowingly breaking the law. Mr Drury has chosen not to take advantage of this and you may ask yourselves, why? I put forward a possible reason, which you are free to accept or reject. He wished to be tried on a charge of perjury in the glare of publicity since he had previously suffered very considerable *adverse* publicity and believed this case would enable him to regain his moral innocence. His decision may be regarded as a gamble. It is you, members of the jury, who will decide whether he gambled wisely.'

The jury did not retire. Those on the outside of the two rows of seats stood, in order to speak to those in the centre. Their buzz of hurried conversation was audible, but not the words. Soon, they regained their ordered positions.

'Members of the jury, have you reached a unanimous verdict?'

'We have,' replied the standing chairman.

'What is your verdict?'

'Not guilty.'

There was some cheering, quickly subdued.

Outside the courtroom, her eyes tearful, Diana hugged Drury.
'Steve, Steve, I died a thousand deaths when the judge said
you had gambled.'

'I held a royal flush.'

'Right then, it looked like a busted straight.' She did not
believe in a public display of affection, but she kissed him.